A native of Devon, David Rees is the author of many novels, including some for young people, and of several works of literary criticism. In 1978 he won the Carnegie Medal for *The Exeter Blitz*, and in 1980 The Other Award for *The Green Bough of Liberty*. His other books published by GMP include *The Hunger* and *The Estuary*.

David Rees

First published March 1982 by Gay Men's Press, P.O. Box 247, London N15 6RW
Fourth impression 1989

British Library/Library of Congress Cataloguing in Publication Data
   Rees, David
     The milkman's on his way.
     I. Title
     823' 914[F]   PR6058.E/

     ISBN 0 907040 12 8

The quotation on p. 6 is from W.H. Auden, *Collected Poems*
(ed. Edward Mendelson), and is reproduced with kind
permission of Faber and Faber Ltd. (UK) and Random
House Inc. (US).

Printed in the European Community by
Nørhaven A/S, Viborg, Denmark

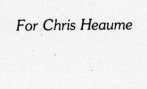
For Chris Heaume

About suffering they were never wrong,
The Old Masters: how well they understood
Its human position; how it takes place
While someone else is eating or opening a window
    or just walking dully along.

W.H. Auden, *Musée des Beaux Arts*

One: The Meningitis Summer

The summer I was fifteen I had meningitis. I don't know how I contracted the disease, but a few days before I became ill Leslie and I had been poking around in a drain at the back of the shop where his mother worked. She had seen a rat scuttling into it. Mum was convinced that was the cause, but I'm not sure she's right: Leslie didn't get meningitis. I was unconscious a lot of the time, and when I wasn't, I was vomiting and experiencing headaches so painful I sometimes screamed aloud. While Leslie was on the beach, swimming, surfing, and giving himself a superb suntan over as much of his body as he dared to expose. Which meant there wasn't much trace of white! But his good luck and my aches and agonies aren't the reason I'm starting here; it's because during my illness I noticed something about my mother I hadn't been aware of previously. 'That we should suffer this!' she said to me one morning. The pronoun was peculiar, I thought, a few minutes later when the remark had sunk in: it was *I* who was suffering. And I remembered she had said more or less the same thing twice before, but in my fever the words had floated over me and not registered.

When she brought to my bedside some little delicacy she had cooked, broth or an egg custard or a milk pudding — foods the doctor had said I would be able to keep down — and I refused to touch them because even the suggestion of something to eat was utterly nauseous, the hurt she obviously experienced made me feel so guilty that I tried to swallow a spoonful just to please her. And immediately threw up.

'What can I do?' she asked on one of these occasions, as she mopped the sick from my chin and my lips. 'What more can I do? I've tried everything!'

I closed my eyes, wishing she would go away. It was easier for me, she seemed to be hinting, than it was for her: all I had to do was lie there while she suffered helplessly.

I thought about this, on and off, during the next few weeks as I recovered and took my first shaky steps out of doors, and walked for the first time since my illness down to the beach and watched Leslie laughing in the sea. Some heavy responsibility had been laid on me; I had discovered some tangled knot in the web of feeling that existed between us, but I wasn't sure what it was. Maybe my purpose, in her view, was to bring her joy, pride, and achievement: sorrow was prohibited. Leslie came running across the sand. The smooth golden skin, the muscles that worked in every part of his body seemingly without effort, even the long fair hair made me envious. After my sickness I was pitifully thin and white; it would take years, as it so happened, to recover that lost flesh — but I was also aware that I admired his appearance too: he was strikingly good-looking. I felt a shiver inside. Of pleasure; but also ill omen, as if a cloud had just blotted out sunlight. I knew, at that moment, that I'd bring my mother more sorrow than joy, though what the nature of that sorrow might be I hadn't the faintest idea.

I remembered that when she had brought me that broth, that egg custard, she had been wearing her rings. As people do in moments of drama or ceremony, a friend's wedding, or on board a sinking ship while waiting for rescue.

But we got on well enough. As well as any teenage kid gets on with his mum, which meant our only arguments were over coming in at night later than she said I should. And riding on the back of Little Michael's motorbike: areas of behaviour in which she thought I'd hurt myself or be killed. But Dad said nothing. And when he found out that I'd been in pubs with Leslie, that I smoked cigarettes occasionally, he simply remarked that as long as I paid for my own pleasures he didn't mind; I was old enough, in his opinion, to decide whether I wanted to rot my lungs with tobacco smoke or not. And going to discos with girls — well, that was all right too. Not that I spent every one of my free hours indulging in such activities: I liked the company of my parents. Helping Dad with the garden or with jobs round the house was fun: I enjoyed working with him and chatting about nothing in particular.

Dad is a milkman. He's luckier than some; he doesn't have to get up in the middle of the night to start his job. Eight a.m. he begins. Not in the town; it's a country route — all the little villages and outlying cottages south-east of Bude. Some of the people don't get their milk till four o'clock in the afternoon, which is a bit silly when you remember they live, many of them, a stone's throw from a farm. But that's how it is these days: the farmer milks the cows at the crack of dawn, a lorry transports the stuff to the dairy, it's processed and bottled, then Dad takes it back, half a day later, to people who live on the other side of the hedge from the field where the cows are eating the grass. Progress, Dad sarcastically calls it: modernisation, efficiency. When I was younger I used to go with him, during the holidays when I had nothing better to do, or if he needed a helping hand. He doesn't like the work very much. 'When you trot off into the big wide world and earn your own living,' he often said, 'make sure it's got more prospects than this. This is a dead-end job.' Strange. I've always found it quite pleasant. No boss breathing down your neck; and the countryside early on a summer morning is, as far as working conditions are concerned, as satisfying as anything one could want.

I got teased about it at school, however; that year the old song *Lullaby of Broadway* was revived and zoomed up the charts. When the kids saw me coming they'd call out 'The milkman's on his way!' which they seemed to think was very funny; then they'd quote things from the adverts on telly, like 'Don't forget your daily pinta!' and 'Are *you* getting enough?' That last remark especially annoyed me, as the first time I heard it the sexual implication made me blush bright red. If you're pale, and have freckles and gingerish brown curls as I have, you'll know that blushing makes you look much more embarrassed than if you've got a dark skin and jet black hair. So of course they said that more often than the other comments. I wasn't, as it happens, getting enough in that sense; indeed I wasn't getting anything at all. Nor were they. But we'd reached the age when we talked about it a great deal, Leslie in particular. Any good-looking girl we passed on the road or saw on the beach, he'd stare after her and say it shouldn't be allowed, such temptation. To me, he seemed obsessed, as if he was walking around with a non-stop erection three miles high. I was puzzled: girls didn't have that effect on me at all. Which bothered me slightly. They *ought* to have some effect; I could see that, because all the other boys reacted like Leslie, even if they didn't say as much as he did. But I was re-assured a little when I read in a book that people didn't necessarily develop in that way at the same speed.

After I had recovered from my illness and was more or less fit enough to lead a normal life again, I found a change in people's relationships. When Leslie and I weren't doing things on our own we went around with four other boys — John Anderson, Alan Carter, John Whitton who was called Bookworm John to distinguish him from the other John, and little Michael Wade who was a year older than we were and more or less our leader as he had a motorbike. John Anderson was called Wimpy John because he'd just started work at the local Wimpy bar; he was also a year older. Bookworm John wasn't really a bookworm. He'd been given that nickname after we'd found him in the school library one day browsing through Plato's *Symposium*. He'd been reading it, he assured us, not because he was remotely turned on by the Ancient Greeks, but because someone had told him it was all about sex. Very disappointing too, he added; it only described poofs, men having sex with other men. He put it back on the library shelf. I didn't bother to look at it. It hadn't occurred to me, then, that the subject-matter was something I'd find, later, of enormous importance and interest.

What I found had changed was that instead of talking about

women, the others had actually taken some practical steps in that direction. We were still a gang, but it had doubled in size. There were six girls: Molly, Juicy Lucy, Linda, Adrienne, Karen, and Louise. Everyone was more or less paired off, Molly with Alan, Michael with Lucy, Leslie with Linda. Adrienne and Karen, who were best friends, were supposed to be with the two Johns, though it seemed fairly clear that they weren't really ready for this sort of thing: they preferred to spend their time giggling with each other rather than being alone with Bookworm or Wimpy. Which left Louise. Who was meant to be for me, I assumed. She didn't look any more or less attractive than the other girls. A bit on the fat side, with big dark eyes.

We'd go to the beach and the cinema, all twelve of us, but mostly, in the evenings, because there was nowhere else and none of us had any money, we'd sit in John's Wimpy bar, trying to make a cup of coffee stretch out for an hour without being forced to buy another. We'd leave, not in a bunch, but in twos. On the way home, I'd put my arm round Louise and kiss her. Not particularly because I wanted to — it never, once, excited me — but because it was expected. She expected it, and doubtless all the others were doing it, and... hadn't everything we'd ever talked about or read or seen on the telly or in the cinema suggested that this was normal and desirable; what all girls and boys wanted? But to me it was a very over-rated pastime. Dead boring.

Leslie, when I saw him on his own, talked incessantly about Linda. How far she'd let him go. (Almost nowhere, it seemed.) When he asked me about Louise, I was very evasive. But I admitted, eventually, that we had done nothing, and that the idea of doing so didn't particularly fill me with uncontrolled sexual desire.

He stared at me. 'What's the matter with you?' he asked. 'Are you queer or something?'

Was I? I wondered if it might be possible, but I tried to push the idea out of my head: it was too awful to consider. I'd never met anybody who was, and a queer to me was a figure of fun, pathetic and silly, like Mr Humphreys on *Are You Being Served?* I didn't want to be like that. I *wasn't* like that! But what was I? I didn't know. If I was a poof it would be the end of the world. I'd have to hide it from my parents and all my friends. I'd never do anything about it, not in a million years! Then I thought of Louise with no clothes on, of the two of us making love. The image was repellent, so totally undesirable that just the idea of it made me feel physically ill. I glanced at Leslie. He was a damn sight better-looking than Louise. And I started to imagine me and Leslie . . .

I went back to the book that said people developed at different speeds. Homosexuals, it told me, were sick people who, even if society unjustly persecuted them, were perpetually unhappy and dissatisfied. But on one point I felt re-assured: all teenagers, it said, went through a homosexual phase. It was part of the turmoil of adolescence. That must be it, I decided. A healthy interest in girls would come later. It didn't occur to me that this little sex manual — written especially for young people, and given to me by my parents — might be wrong on all these counts, though I did have enough intelligence to hesitate over the statement about *all* teenagers going through a homosexual phase. Everybody I knew, boys and girls, appeared to have taken to heterosexual behaviour as ducks to water. Or were they having similar problems to mine, but hiding them so cleverly that the rest of us had no inkling? It was unlikely. None of my friends was capable of being as secretive as that. Or were they? But I kept my anxieties very much bottled up inside. Leslie? Impossible! Perhaps it was just *some* people, not everybody as the book said. Though why the hell did it have to be me?

But life wasn't one long round of worry. I quite enjoyed Louise's company, and she was not all that bothered, as far as the physical side of the relationship was concerned, that I didn't want to do anything more than hold hands or kiss her goodnight. In fact, she was rather relieved. Perhaps all the girls would have been relieved: Linda, certainly, wasn't ready for more than that. Which caused arguments and tension between her and Leslie. Maybe, I began to think to myself, I was better off than he was. It was fun, the gang of us, going around together. Having a girl-friend made me feel equal with the other boys, conferred on me a kind of status. Leslie, however, wasn't interested in status; he couldn't have cared less about the gang. For him, it was simply more pleasant than being alone. What he wanted was Linda to himself, just the two of them; but that situation, even if deep down she liked the thought of it, she considered dangerous.

And there was school work to occupy my mind. With September our last year started, C.S.E. exams looming closer and closer as the months went by. My illness meant I had missed almost a whole term's work. I tried hard to catch up. But I wasn't very bright, academically, and I felt pretty certain I wouldn't do well. Not well enough, that is, to escape the fate allotted to most teenagers in a place like Bude, which had no industries of any sort: unemployment. There wasn't a factory for miles around. All you could hope for, if you weren't brilliant, was a casual job in the cafes and hotels during the summer.

Dad nagged me a little about this. 'You ought to think carefully about what you want to do when you leave,' he said.

'I have thought,' I answered. 'But I don't know whether there's any choice.'

'Mrs Davis's son is doing very well,' Mum said. 'You know — Peter Davis. He left school last year, didn't he?'

'Yes. With five "O" levels.' Peter Davis worked in a solicitor's office. It was not the kind of job I wanted, indoors and desk-bound, and Peter Davis, a dull, shy kid whose face was studded with acne, wasn't a person I looked up to in any way.

Mum sighed. 'A great pity you never got onto the "O" level course,' she said.

'No, it isn't.' Dad came to my defence.' "O" levels and all that sort of caper aren't suitable for everybody. Don't give the boy an inferiority complex. He does his best.'

'I *am* trying,' I told her.

'I'm sure you are,' she said. 'But I wish you hadn't missed nearly a whole term last year.'

'It couldn't be helped.'

'Be thankful he didn't die,' Dad said.

I laughed. 'I had no intention of snuffing it!'

'Go on doing your best. That's all we want.'

Mum said that that was all she wanted too, but she didn't sound so convinced. I felt close to my father at that time. During the Christmas and Easter holidays I helped him on his milk-round: we never talked about anything very much, nothing like the discussions and arguments I sometimes had with Louise or Leslie, but the hours passed pleasantly enough, dissecting last night's TV programmes, or the strange lives of some of the people to whom we delivered the milk. Sometimes he'd mention Mum, never serious criticisms, but his remarks about her being too house-proud, or feeling scared of horses and pigs, or disapproving of the Benny Hill show, suggested that he and I, the males of the family, had a sort of alliance that might come in useful when feminine ideas and opinions went too far. And our silences — long and frequent — weren't embarrassed black holes in the conversation, with both of us trying frantically to think of something to say, but were warm and companionable: we knew each other sufficiently well to know when it simply wasn't necessary to talk.

Dad read the *Sun* every day, mostly the sports section. He took it with him on his round, and sometimes I would find him ogling the girl on page three. 'A right little cracker,' he said on one occasion. 'Isn't she?'

I had a good look: it was expected. As was my agreeing with his assessment. But she did nothing for me; she was just so much bare flesh. A girl with extremely large tits. So what? I felt uneasy. It was bad enough, living a life of pretence with Louise, Leslie, and the others; but I had learned to cope with that. Now it seemed to be intruding into other areas of my existence: would I be able to get by? I'd be found out. That was my worst fear.

He put the newspaper away, and started to talk about whether Exeter City would keep their place in the third division next season. That was the end, I hoped, of showing me that he liked page three of the *Sun* and assuming that I did too. But I was wrong. On subsequent mornings, I was often asked for my views on the girl of the day. 'I wouldn't turn *her* down,' was his comment on one of these creatures, who was sticking her bottom out in a

14

supposedly provocative manner. I thought she looked quite revolting.

'Dad, I didn't know you were a sex maniac,' I said, lightly. 'Whatever would Mum say?'

'It's natural, isn't it?'

I imagined it was. For everyone in the world, it seemed, except me. 'What's wrong with Mum?'

'Nothing.' My question surprised him. 'Nothing at all. What made you ask that?'

'I wasn't being serious.'

'I should hope not, indeed! Your mother and I are very happily married. Always have been. Never any trouble between us of that sort. But there's no harm in looking at a picture. We're all human, aren't we?'

'Oh yes.'

He laughed. 'I'm not one of those old fuddy-duddies who've forgotten what it was like to be fifteen. I should say nearly sixteen: only two months now to your birthday. Good God! It makes me feel old!'

We had arrived at the village of Marhamchurch, which I hoped would bring an end to this topic of conversation. There was work to do, leaving the correct number of bottles outside each house, he taking one side of the road and me the other. He would surely come back to the van with something else on his mind: Mrs Powelsland's youngest girl had been ill yesterday, and he'd have news of whether she was better or worse or much the same; Mrs Oke wanted two extra pints because she had visitors arriving, and Dad would tell me whether it was her brother and his family or her parents-in-law; Mr Honeychurch had run off with someone else's wife a few weeks ago, and Mrs Honeychurch was now carrying on with a lad of seventeen who milked the cows at Fuidge Farm, but this lad was also carrying on with a girl from Whitstone who was no better than she should be, and Mrs Honeychurch had caught them, red-handed, on Saturday night: Dad would undoubtedly give me a progress report on that particular shemozzle.

But he didn't. As we drove up the road towards Bridgerule, he said 'How are you getting on with Louise these days?'

'What do you mean,' I asked, guardedly, 'how are we getting on?'

'Nothing special. You seem to spend a lot of your free time with her.'

'When I ought to be studying?'

'I didn't say that. All work and no play makes Jack a dull boy. No . . . I just wondered . . . if . . .'

'If what?'

'If everything was all right. No need to get so prickly about it! I was only asking a friendly question.'

Help! I thought. He wonders if we've been to bed together! 'She's just someone to go around with,' I told him. 'There's nothing in it at all. Absolutely nothing.'

He smiled, then went on, as if he hadn't taken in a single word I'd been saying, 'It's not very easy at your age . . . controlling your feelings . . . I'm always here if you want to ask my advice. You do know that, Ewan, don't you?'

'Of course.'

I stared out of the window at the passing fields, acutely embarrassed. Was he trying to say something about contraceptives? It would be so good, so really good, to tell him exactly what was troubling me, to hear him say it didn't matter, that he understood, that it was a phase he'd been through himself; but he wouldn't: he'd be appalled. If this went on, I suddenly realised, if it wasn't something I could grow out of, I'd be cut off — for ever maybe — from my parents in one of the most important areas of life. It was too bleak even to contemplate. 'Tell me about Mrs Honeychurch,' I said, wanting to return to the safe, ordinary topics of our conversations. 'Has Gilbert made his peace with her? Given up the Whitstone girl? Or is he having it away with somebody else?'

When exams were over Leslie and I hardly bothered to attend school. The weather was magnificent and as the beach was only ten minutes' walk from home our days were spent swimming and surfing. June, July. I spent much more of my time with Leslie than with Louise. She wasn't particularly interested in the sea, like so many people who are brought up within sight and sound of it, whereas he and I often said it was the only thing that made existence in Bude just about tolerable. He had abandoned Linda and was after other girls. Something struck him that had been obvious to me for ages: women found him good-looking, attractive, and sexy. He could choose almost any girl he wanted. And the ones he was interested in now let him go a bit further than Linda had. Though not as far as he hoped, he admitted when I pressed him on the subject, not far enough by a long chalk. Which, he said, in the end was less satisfactory than Linda: he got frantically worked up and there was no relief whatsoever. Except by himself, he said, grinning shyly, as if he was introducing into the conversation something that shouldn't be mentioned; it was, he added, a stage he would like to leave behind. Women! They were holding him back, frustrating him, preventing him from moving into the next department of life. 'What about you?' he asked.

'Me? Oh . . . I've nothing to report.'

He was silent. Then said 'You're a dark horse, Ewan.'

The summer heatwave seemed to go on for ever. We wore only shorts and sandals, and even that, most of the day, was too much: we were constantly plunging into the sea just to cool off. We both began to take a serious interest in surfing. We'd been able to use a board for years, from almost the time we could swim; I can hardly remember when we couldn't. But until now it had been merely a pastime, just fun to wrestle with the swell or flirt with danger, enjoying the sensation of excitement as we shot towards the beach ahead of a really good wave. Now we began to look at it as a particular kind of skill, one which we wanted to learn to the best of our abilities. We had both asked for, and got, new malibu boards for our sixteenth birthdays. Bude is a surf town, though not as popular as it used to be. The sea is often excellent, as good as anywhere in England, but treacherous currents can make even swimming impossible, particularly at low tide. And the beaches face only one way — west — whereas further down the coast, at Newquay for instance, there are three different directions owing to the structure of the cliffs and the positions of the headlands, so that if the surf is poor at one place it is more than likely good or first class at the others. 'Next year, if I can, I shall spend the whole summer at Newquay,' Leslie said one morning, when we found ourselves staring at water as flat and useless as a millpond.

We read books on the subject. And joined the local Surf Club. We became almost fanatical about it; we could hardly talk of anything else. My parents must have found us extremely boring. 'Make the most of it,' Mum said. 'The long hot summer won't last for ever.' She was trying to be particularly nice to me: C.S.E. results had arrived. I hadn't done at all well. Nor had Leslie. We went down to the social security together and signed on. There were few jobs available. We tried for what seemed within our capabilities, but none of the bosses wanted to know. A few even laughed.

So, more concentration on surfing. We improved, rapidly. And started to experiment with the more difficult and spectacular techniques: going in the tube (which means allowing the wave to curl right over you) or trying a spinner (you whisk the board round in a 180 degree turn) or a side slide (you come down the wave parallel to it instead of at an angle). Leslie was stronger than me, a heavier sort of person. He could conquer waves I wouldn't even dare to attempt, but I was the first to execute a perfect spinner and master the skill of the side slide. I had more finesse, he said, a greater delicacy. We wanted to try our luck in a championship; neither of us would win, of course, but we would have liked to find out where we stood. There wasn't such an event for juniors, however, on the calendar at Bude.

Leslie said we needed to build up our strength if we were to improve any more. Swimming and surfing were not enough; they didn't cater for all the body's muscles. We ought to go for a four-mile run every day or cycle twenty miles; we should do various gymnastic exercises and take up weight-lifting. 'If we did all that,' I said, 'we'd have no time in the sea! Anyway, my bike is bust.'

'We could go jogging. And there's a gym club we could join. Look at your arms!' He gripped my biceps. 'You see? Flabby. The girls won't like that.'

'Flabby biceps? I don't think it's the sort of thing that worries them.'

'Oh, that's all you know about it,' he said, loftily.

'You reckon girls like a beefcake type of body? Mr Universe?'

'Well . . . not Mr Universe exactly. But a bit of muscle wouldn't look out of place.'

'No. I suppose not.' I rather liked the idea. I'd found, recently, that my eyes kept straying to the tough, well-built men on the beach. They held my attention; and returned to my mind when I was thinking about something else. I didn't interpret this interest as raging sexual desire; it seemed to me that I admired and envied them, as I did Leslie. I wanted to be like them. Even to *be* them. Which was stupid; in fact inexplicable, I told myself one evening as I looked at my own body in the bathroom mirror. There was nothing dreadfully wrong or misshapen with my own physique, though it was still very thin. There was no lack of muscle. And I was tremendously suntanned. What was wrong with me? Did I *fancy* these men? Leslie? As I should a girl? I just didn't know. And as usual, I pushed the problem out of my head as best I could. My days were filled and happy; Leslie's company was all I wanted, and the hot summer nights, meeting the others at the Wimpy bar, or wandering around the town in a group and dancing at the occasional disco, were fun too.

So we practised weight-lifting, Leslie and I, twice a week at the gym. And we went out before breakfast, jogging. Not four miles of it as he had suggested, not even three. Round the edge of the golf links, a big green triangle of open space just behind the beach; on two of its sides were houses and hotels, on the other the cliff road. Then a sprint, racing each other flat out to see who could be first. Sometimes he won, sometimes it was me: on one occasion a dead heat, each of us trying to jostle the other as we pushed open the back door of my house, then dash through the kitchen, up the stairs, and into my bedroom, which we'd agreed beforehand was 'home.' I shoved him away from me in the hall, shot up to the landing, and threw myself, exhausted and panting, onto my bed. He pounded up after me, yelling 'You ratbag!', then flopped down beside me. Silence, except for frantic gulping of breath. Our legs touched. Sweat. Then the most extraordinary, unlooked for, incredible thing happened. His hand was inside my shorts.

For me, though not for him, it was one of the most important moments of my life: a revelation: nothing had told me so much about myself before, or was ever to spell it out so clearly again.

I tugged at his shorts; I wanted to see. 'What the hell do you think you're doing?' he asked. But changed his mind: they were obviously a handicap. He shut his eyes. I did not, amazed at what I saw. I hadn't realised how much the size of an erect cock differed from one person to another. Noticing other boys, limp in the changing-room at school, had merely told me mine was much the same as other people's. But Leslie's was a prodigy. Would a girl be able to cope with such a weapon?

I wanted to touch him, caress him, wrap myself round him, kiss him all over. I didn't, of course. He was doubtless pretending that my hand was Linda's or Adrienne's or whoever the girl of the moment was, and I . . . I saw only him. The climax was the most ecstatic few seconds I had ever experienced.

He opened his eyes. 'What are you smiling at?' he asked. His words were loud and harsh; they seemed to tear the silence to shreds and break the spell utterly.

'Nothing.' I made my mouth look stern. 'Maybe . . . we shouldn't have done that.' I didn't mean what I said, but I guessed such a comment was what he expected me to say. It would have been catastrophic if I'd let him know how much I'd enjoyed it.

'Probably not,' he agreed. He rolled off the bed and picked up his tee-shirt and shorts. 'It doesn't matter,' he said. 'Does it? Better than the solitary thing. I get so frustrated . . . If only I could find a girl, just *one* girl, who'd let me!' I didn't answer. 'You're not angry, are you?'

'Angry? No, not at all.'

'I was worried you might be. That you'd be so livid or something you wouldn't want to speak to me again. I mean . . . I started it.'

'I didn't stop you.' Then, as he looked at me with a slightly odd expression, I added, lying through my teeth, 'I've got the same problems as you have.'

'Oh? Louise?'

'Well...you know...'

He was dressed now. 'I feel...a bit bad about it, all the same.'

I shrugged my shoulders. 'It's not the end of the world. It happened; that's all. It's of no significance.'

He nodded. 'Just physical relief, I suppose. Bloody women! Well...I'm going home. Bath and breakfast.'

'Shall I call for you later? The sea should be good this morning.'

'Yes. Give me an hour.'

I listened to him clatter down the stairs, and heard the door slam shut behind him. The silence surged back, so thick it was almost tangible, like velvet.

A revelation, I said. Now I *knew*. Knew for a certainty that I'd never enjoy it so much with a girl. It couldn't, it just wouldn't be possible. I wasn't in a 'phase'. I was homosexual. And always had been. And always would be.

But I was far from ready to be happy about that. I was *terrified*.

And wanting Leslie all over again. I'd not ask, not even suggest or hint at such a thing. It would have to happen exactly as it had done just now, spontaneously, he starting it. Any move on my part and I would be exposed for what I was, with all the dire and dreadful consequences such knowledge in the hands of others would bring down on me.

Sperm on my skin, his mixed with mine. I touched it, then licked my finger. I was still perpendicular, firm as a rock; a situation I *could* do something about, and I did, reliving the experience in my imagination.

Two: The Linga Longa Cafe

One curious result of what happened was that, for a time, I drew closer to my mother. I remembered that moment on the beach the previous year when I felt I'd bring her more sorrow than joy; then, I didn't know why I felt that, or how it would come about. Now I knew. If she discovered what I was she'd never forgive me. Nor, maybe, herself: she'd think she was responsible, that something in the way she had brought me up had caused this dreadful thing. Thing? What name would she give it? Disease? Crime? Neurosis? Some such word, certainly. I thought about that a lot. What had caused it, what 'it' really was. Disease was absurd. So was crime. I didn't feel in the least bit ill. Or criminal. And I wasn't a screaming neurotic. There was nothing very terrible that she had done to me in early childhood; growing up had been easy. My parents had never ill-treated me or made excessive demands. Nor had they dressed me up as a girl or stopped me from indulging in normal boys' pastimes and interests.

I began to be more considerate to Mum: it was like paying cash into the bank in order to fend off some future crisis. Saving for the proverbial rainy day. She worked in a shop in Kilkhampton Street, selling cakes and loaves of bread. Which, of course, was why the house had been empty when Leslie and I had returned from jogging, why our escapade had been possible. I had grown used, when quite young, to having the house to myself in the mornings and afternoons of the school holidays, to cooking my own breakfast and lunch. Now, when she returned from the shop tired out, I would, if I was in, make her a pot of tea and tell her to put her feet up, or in the evening bring her a cup of coffee while she watched the television. I wiped the dishes without being asked, and on two or three occasions I actually did the ironing.

'Are you about to put in a request for something big, Ewan?'

'No.'

'I was wondering why you've started being so thoughtful.'

'No reason in particular . . . You look a bit under the weather.'

'I have been more tired than usual this past fortnight, to tell the truth.'

Dad glanced up from his paper. 'I hadn't noticed,' he said.

'Oh, you never notice anything!' she replied, scornfully.

'You're not ill, are you?' He began to sound anxious.

'No, no. We're just extra busy at the shop; that's all. There seem to be more holiday-makers this summer than any year I can remember.'

'Yes. There are.' He returned to the sports page. 'Good training for Ewan,' he said. 'Make somebody a nice little housewife one of these days.' He laughed.

My heart nearly missed a beat. What did he mean by that? Had he guessed?

'What a thing to say!' my mother exclaimed, affecting to be shocked.

'No, I meant it,' Dad said. 'The whole world's different from when we were young, what with women's lib and all that sort of caper. When we got married we knew where we stood; some jobs belonged to the men and some to the women. Ewan's wife will probably want him to make beds and change nappies and do the shopping while she goes out to work. That's how it is now. I'm right, Ewan, aren't I?'

'Could be,' I said, cautiously. I felt somewhat relieved at the turn his thoughts had taken.

'It doesn't do men any harm to be aware of what's involved in running a house,' my mother said. 'If I had a stroke and got carted off to hospital, you wouldn't know how to survive! Lord! You don't even know how to boil an egg properly!'

My father filled his pipe and lit it. This was something he often did when he was at a loss for words; it gave him time to think. 'I do know how to boil an egg properly,' he said, as he blew out dense clouds of smoke. 'And if you think I should do women's work, why aren't you rushing to learn how to do my jobs? Can you mend a puncture? Put a plug on a piece of flex? Fit a new washer on a tap? Dig the vegetable garden so we have a good crop of peas and beans? You wouldn't know where to begin!'

I could mend punctures and fix tap washers; I could also cook quite reasonably. A mixture. Was that yet another sign? Of course not! It was simply that roles, as far as who does what is concerned, had indeed changed.

'I think this is a stupid conversation,' Mum said. She got up and went into the kitchen.

Dad and I laughed. 'Game, set, and match,' he said. 'Still . . . she's probably right about being tired. I am myself. They say the average milkman shifts about five thousand pints a week. I've never bothered to count, but last week it felt like ten thousand! I was leaving bottles on doorsteps in my sleep, all night long. Not good, that.' He picked up the *Sun* and handed it to me. 'Have an eyeful of page three. Something extra special today.'

I looked at her, and passed it back to him. 'Not bad,' I said.

'Not bad! What's the matter with you? Sometimes I think you're a bit of a prude.'

'Not at all!'

'Found yourself a job yet?'

'They need someone at the Linga Longa Cafe; I'll go down in the morning and see what they want. But if they don't pay more than the dole it's not worth taking. It's only seasonal, of course, till the end of October.'

'It's a start.'

'Yes.'

'You won't be able to spend so much time in the sea.'

'Surfing's all very well, but it doesn't bring in any money.'

'I'm told you're becoming quite an expert. I'm glad.' He smiled, pleased to find something in his son to be proud of. If you knew the truth, I said to myself, you'd probably want to kick me out of the house.

Was there a cure for it? I went to the library and searched for something that might help. I didn't take the books out; no explanation I could think of would sound convincing if my mother saw in my bedroom a treatise on homosexuality. Even reading in the reference section of the library was a furtive and surreptitious act; suppose the girl at the desk saw the titles? My mother knew her. And gossip travels very fast in Bude.

There wasn't much on the subject. The local powers that be evidently didn't seem to think it a matter of burning interest to the inhabitants of North Cornwall. But the few snippets of information I did gather, from psychology books and sex primers, all told me the same thing: there was no cure. About the cause of it they tended to disagree, which surprised me: didn't people really know? And *why* didn't they know? It had been around, I discovered, for as long as mankind had existed. Had people been so irresponsible that they could never be bothered to find out? Most of the authors were emphatic that seduction by someone of your own sex was not the cause; they argued that it was the result of having an overbearing mother and a weak or absent father in the case of homosexual boys, the opposite with girls: for some inexplicable reason, the children of such marriages found it difficult or impossible to model themselves on the parent of their own sex. But one author argued very strongly that if this theory was correct, then *all* children of these marriages would be homosexual, and the evidence tended to suggest that this wasn't so. There were sometimes identical twins where one was gay and the other was not, and vast numbers of homosexuals from marriages that didn't consist of hen-pecked husbands and wives who wore the trousers. Gay: it was the first time I had heard this word. My parents' marriage, certainly, was normal; whatever 'normal' implied — I was beginning to have doubts about its meaning: it no longer seemed to convey anything very coherent. This particular writer said man would discover the causes of homosexuality when he discovered the

25

causes of heterosexuality, and went on to say that asking such questions was fundamentally absurd. More relevant, he thought, would be to find out why society had always disliked and persecuted gay people: an attitude or emotion he called 'homophobia.' I was, to some extent, relieved. I didn't want to think my parents had made me like this. It didn't seem fair. Or was I just looking for a reason, an excuse even, not to blame my parents because I loved them? Perhaps. But I don't think so. I was like this, quite regardless of anything they'd ever done. And would have been had they brought me up in an absolutely different way.

Why did people persecute homosexuals? Society, I read, always needed scapegoats. Jews. Blacks. Hitler had incarcerated homosexuals and forced them to wear a pink triangle on their clothes, just as the Jews had been ordered to wear the star of David. Half a million gays had died at Auschwitz, Belsen, and other concentration camps. Loving your own sex, in the opinion of most of the human race, was unnatural, disgusting, and sterile. Probably its unproductiveness was, more than anything else, the reason why it was persecuted. A gay relationship didn't produce children, didn't propagate the species. It appeared, to those with a puritanical cast of mind, to be sex simply for pleasure, an evasion of responsibilities, a threat to the basic unit out of which the entire fabric of society was structured: the family.

One in ten people was, wholly or in part, homosexual. Five *million* in the United Kingdom! Where were they all? Hidden, presumably, as I was, under a heterosexual facade. As far as I was aware I was the only one in Bude. According to the statistics, there should be hundreds!

But, as I returned the books to the library shelves, I felt sadness rather than relief. The feelings expressed in what I had read, with the exception of the author who had stated that the cause of homosexuality was an irrelevant question, were either pitying, patronising or more or less condemnatory. I didn't want pity, patronage, or condemnation. I wanted to be told . . . what? That there was nothing wrong with me, I think. Be gay and happy. I didn't realise that *I* was the only person who could tell myself that

that was so. The only authority.

The Linga Longa Cafe decided to employ me. Waiting at the tables, washing up, sweeping the floor, anything that needed doing except sitting on my backside at the cash-desk. The manageress did that. The hours were helpful from my point of view, eleven a.m. till three p.m., then in the evenings from half past six till half past ten; which meant there was time during the day for surfing. The cafe became so busy in the second half of August that the manageress had to take on another person. Leslie got the job.

The work was boring, hard, and not very lucrative, though the pay was certainly better than being on the dole. And they gave us our lunch and an evening meal. As we didn't finish till half past ten, there weren't a great many places open in which we could waste our hard-earned money. I bought some new clothes — jeans, a decent shirt, shoes. Mum took a couple of quid for my keep, which was ridiculously small, but she said I wasn't earning a fortune, and, besides, she was spending less on the housekeeping as I ate at the cafe. Leslie saved his up for weeks and eventually, in October, he bought a wet suit: prices had dropped as the surfing season neared its end.

We were together now, he and I, almost from the time we got out of bed in the mornings till we slept at night, for we continued to go for our run and surf in the afternoons; and on Saturdays, when the pubs stayed open till eleven, we'd drink two or three pints of beer before going home. (Saturday was pay day.) I liked the arrangement: I preferred to be with Leslie than with anybody else I knew. But he wasn't always happy. Not that he seemed to get fed up with my company: it was more a question of lacking the time to pursue the opposite sex. In his third week at the cafe, however, he struck up a friendship with one of the waitresses, Sandra, a dreary, plain girl who, I guessed, might give him everything he asked for. After work now I went home on my own while he took Sandra for a stroll on the cliffs.

'She's a slut,' I told him.

'So much the better,' was his answer. 'But how do you know?'

'I don't. I just think she looks like one.'

27

'Does she?'

'You mean you haven't found out yet?'

'No.'

Which I knew anyway. By tacit agreement our early morning run no longer ended with my bedroom as the winning-post; but we had had sex again. More than once; several times in fact, and it always started in the same way, with Leslie the initiator. Neither of us ever said a word to each other about it; his first remark, when it was over, was usually 'I'd better go home and change' or I would say 'I must get myself something to eat.' I acted as casually as he did, as if to reinforce his opinion that it was of the utmost irrelevance; but I was always worried that my face or my body would give me away by reflecting the intense pleasure I felt every time.

I began to wonder about him. Why did he want to do it? What *really* was going on in his head? Surely some of the girls he had been out with, one or two of them at least, wouldn't object to doing for him as much as I did, tossing him off. It would hardly make them pregnant. Or were they scared that if they went that far, he'd want more, the whole thing? That *they'd* want the whole thing? It was possible. Or, when he was alone with a girl, did his normally confident, cheerful, extrovert self vanish; did he become shy, tongue-tied, so nervous that he didn't dare go beyond kissing her goodnight? It was improbable, to judge from the Leslie I had always known, but it could be the explanation. Or was he actually like me, one of those millions of hidden, buried gays? Or bisexual? If that were so, he might fancy me as I did him. Wouldn't I have some inkling, some sign, however small? Not necessarily. *He* hadn't a clue about *me*. We'd had sex now at least a dozen times, and he still hadn't the faintest idea. As far as I knew. It was, I decided eventually, an insoluble mystery, and it would remain so unless I came out into the open, and that, unless I was being excruciatingly tortured, I would never do.

One Saturday evening we went into a crowded pub. (Sandra had gone home early, suffering from a migraine.) Near us was a large party of drinkers, all talking very loudly, as if they wanted the entire bar to hear what they were saying. Everyone addressed everyone else as 'darling', even the men when they spoke to each other; there was a lot of wild embracing, kissing, gushing, and showing off. It was like watching a play. Then I remembered that the actors from the theatre in Exeter were performing all week in Bude: it must be them.

The focus of attention was a tall, slim young man with dark hair, quite good-looking I thought, who, we gathered from the conversation, was the company's assistant director. His voice was the loudest, almost a shriek, and his words virtually an uninterrupted monologue. He had just bought a car, he screamed; wasn't that bold, darling?

'What is it, Crispin?' someone asked.

'Blue, darling.'

Amid the general laughter that followed came the question 'But what *make* is it, Crispin?'

'Make, darling? *I* don't know. I just went in and said I wanted a blue one. Do you think that was wrong? It goes *fearfully* well. I've already driven up three one-way streets in the wrong direction, but, honestly darling, I don't think road signs mean anything serious. Nobody stopped me.'

I nudged Leslie, who was staring open-mouthed in astonishment. 'Poofs!' he said. 'The first I've ever seen in my life!'

'Poofs?'

'Queers! Homos!'

'Are they?' They seemed to me more like actors who, pathetically, had forgotten that the play had finished. It was all so false that you couldn't label it as anything definite like 'homo'.

'Of course they are!' Leslie said. 'Bent as nine-bob bits! Anyone can see that.' He took a long swig of beer. The tone of his voice — scorn and contempt — made me shiver. So that would be what he'd think of his best friend if he knew: I'd been so right, I congratulated myself, on hiding it all away from him.

The assistant director was now giving a soliloquy on the subject of his landlord in Exeter. ' . . . so he said there's some fresh fruit or you could open a tin. I said, darling, I couldn't cope with anything so butch as a *tin*. I mean, what *do* these people expect? It's the same with the light in my bedroom; he thinks I can fathom

29

the mysteries of a two-way switch. I asked the electrician from the theatre to come down and *explain* it all to me, but he wouldn't. Isn't that *amazing*? So I have to go to bed in the dark. *Alone*, darling, *alone*!' Lots of dramatic gestures. 'The theatre is my only mistress, darling!' Slight pause, while he sipped vodka and tonic. 'He said to me one evening he was going to commit suicide. I said, darling, you can't *possibly* do anything so inconsiderate! I'd have to find new lodgings, which would be a *frightful* bore! I said, you really can't expect me to cope with a dead body. I mean, what on earth would I do with it?'

'Let's go,' said Leslie. 'Or I'll have hysterics!' On the way home he ran onto the golf links and yelled at the sky, arms outstretched, 'It's blue, darling! The theatre is my only mistress, darling!' Then he exploded with laughter, jumped up and down, stood on his head, and executed three perfect cartwheels.

When he had sobered a little, I said 'Do you really think they were queer?'

'Of course they were!' And he added, in a less contemptuous tone than he'd used in the pub, 'It's their own business, I suppose. They're not doing any harm.'

Next morning was the only occasion I made any comment on what he and I had done. 'Don't you think,' I asked, 'this . . . you and me just now . . . was queer? More than those actors?'

'Of course not!' There was no hesitation in his answer. 'With us it's simply because our girl-friends won't let us. Does it bother you? If that's the case, we won't do it again.'

'It isn't that.'

'What is it, then?'

'I just thought we haven't any real evidence about that assistant director. For all we know he might be happily married.'

'You do talk a load of balls, Ewan! You can tell them a mile off! Wasn't it obvious? Go on, ask him if he's got a wife and three kids! You'll find there's only one thing he'll be interested in. Your bum.'

'Time for breakfast,' I said. It wasn't a load of balls: in this matter, Leslie was full of confusion and half-baked prejudices, utterly lacking in real knowledge. Where ignorance is bliss . . . there was plenty of truth in that saying.

The following day he was so excited he could hardly contain himself. It had finally happened. With Sandra, on the cliffs. No, not all the way; what he and I did. 'But so incomparably better!' he said. His eyes shone. I'd never seen him looking so happy. 'It was . . . ecstatic! I've got to the next stage at last! I'm growing up!!'

'Bully for you.'

'Can you imagine what it was like, Ewan? Fantastic!'

'Oh, yes. I can imagine.'

'Your turn will come. It isn't a race.'

No, it certainly wasn't a race. And even if it was, I was not one of the competitors. I could see that the moment had arrived when we would begin to grow apart; as he became more involved with the pleasures of heterosexual life, he wouldn't want to take me along with him. Not where one boy and one girl were of the only importance. It wouldn't be Sandra, of course; she was merely a convenience, poor kid. If and when he fell in love I'd lose him altogether. I could look forward to envy and jealousy, watching him approach his rightful inheritance, while I . . . I would stay still. Mark time. There wasn't any inheritance I could see that *I* could approach.

It stopped, the two of us having sex. It was very hard to bear.

At the end of October the cafe jobs finished. We were, both of us, back on the dole. Being almost penniless is much worse when you've had some money in your pocket than it is when you're a kid earning nothing, dependent on Dad for a hand-out. That autumn and winter was a difficult, frustrating, miserable time.

I became a telly addict. I'd had a phase of that once before, when I was about nine. I watched it now all evening, sometimes long after my parents had gone to bed: late shows, late late shows, late late late shows, until the screen went blank and a high-pitched whistle assaulted my ears. Police serials, soap operas, sit coms. And loads of American crap. *Chopper Squad*, which amused me because it was so unbelievably bad: but at least the surf boys were dishy enough to keep my imagination alive. There was nothing else to do. Nothing.

Some of the programmes annoyed me. Anything about teenagers invariably reflected Leslie's way of life, not mine: it was as if being young and homosexual was a problem nobody had ever heard of. Or if they had, it embarrassed them so much they refused to admit that it existed. The adverts were the same. Happy, happy families. None of them seemed to suggest that on planet Earth any other kind of arrangement was possible. Except one about tonic water, of all things; the guy orders his drink in Russian and tells the barmaid he's bilingual. 'Well . . . none of us is perfect,' she says. Then he scowls at her. It made me feel cross. But Mum found it incomprehensible.

'Why does she say that? And why does he look at her so oddly?'

'She thinks he means bisexual,' I informed her.

'Bisexual!'

'Yes.'

It was as if she had never heard the word before. She stared at me, then said 'I don't know where you get such expressions from.'

'It's a quite ordinary word. I don't suppose they'd have it on *Call My Bluff.*'

'What does it mean?'

'That you like men and women equally,' Dad said. 'We had one at the dairy, but he didn't last five minutes!'

Before what, I wondered. I couldn't think of any reason why a bisexual couldn't shift pints of milk. Or a homosexual, for that matter. Or a transvestite. Or a semi-intelligent ape if you trained him carefully. 'What happened to him?' I asked.

'Couldn't stand the teasing.'

'So he left?'

'Yes.'

'Being teased about what?' Mum wanted to know.

Dad and I laughed. 'About liking men as much as women. Haven't you ever heard of such people? He had a wife. And a boyfriend.'

'Oh.' She blushed. 'Yes, I have heard of such people as it so happens. I didn't know there were any in Bude.'

Nor did I. More's the pity. 'They get in everywhere,' Dad said.

'*Everywhere?*' I asked.

'Yes.'

'I'm surprised you know about things like that, Ewan,' she said.

'Honestly, Mum! I wasn't born yesterday! I'll be seventeen in June.'

'Kids know far more these days than is good for them.' She pulled her knitting out from under a cushion, and began to purl and plain with great vigour. A cardigan, pink, a sort of bed-jacket: it was hideous.

I wanted to discover who this man was, but I couldn't think of any way to pursue the conversation without Dad becoming suspicious. I sighed. 'I'm going out,' I said.

'Where to?' Mum asked.

'I don't know. See what Leslie's up to.'

'If you're going far, the pair of you, wrap up well. It's bitterly cold! I was frozen to death at work. There'll be a hard frost tonight.'

'Yes, Mum.' I sighed again.

Leslie was glued to the television, a crummy old Western. He hardly looked up as I came in, and when I spoke his answers were all monosyllables. His mother was out; the cat was occupying her armchair. I shooed it away and sat down, then picked up a magazine from a pile which was lying on the hearth. I turned at once to the help page. I always do; I don't know why: maybe the bits of real life — I'm fourteen and still flat-chested, or my husband has left me for another woman after twenty-seven years of married bliss, or is there some way of removing unsightly hairs from my legs? — seem more interesting than those soppy, boring serials about little Nurse Frump who swoons when the rugged houseman looks at her, or who dreams all day about waltzing off into the sunset with Doctor Gorgeous.

The shock of what I saw written there was so great that the magazine nearly fell out of my hands: a letter from a woman who was disgusted to find examples of homosexual pornography in her eighteen-year-old son's bedroom. Was he sick? Was it her fault? What should she do about it? The answer surprised me even more. 'Do not take such biased views towards homosexuality. Surely you want to see your child grow up happy!

He needs support and understanding, particularly in the extremely difficult area of coming to terms with his sexual orientation. Make use of the various counselling groups. Parents' Enquiry is a good starting-point; it exists specifically to advise and help young homosexuals and their families.' And it gave a phone number.

There were organisations to *help* homosexuals? I was amazed! Staggered would perhaps be a more appropriate word. I memorised the phone number. But . . . would I dare to ring these people? Who were they? What would they want out of me? Would I have to tell them everything about myself? I couldn't do so; it was absolutely impossible!

Ring them, a voice inside me said; ring them!

'I'm off,' I said to Leslie. He waved a hand, but didn't shift his eyes from the television: a dozen baddies were pumping bullets into a lone goodie who was trying to hide behind a moth-eaten cactus. All the bullets missed.

I ran to the nearest phone box, telling myself not to think, not to stop to consider the matter. If I paused for one second my courage would fail; I would never dial that number.

'Hallo. Can I help you?' A woman's voice! It hadn't occurred to me that women would be mixed up in such an organisation.

'Yes. Look . . . er . . . ' I didn't know what to say. What to admit.

'Where are you speaking from?'

'Bude. Bude in Cornwall.'

'That's a long way from here! I wish I knew someone local you could get in touch with, but unfortunately I don't. Never mind; perhaps I can help.'

Silence.

'I won't eat you!' She laughed: a gentle, friendly sound.

I took a deep breath. 'I think . . . I'm gay.'

There was a loud thumping on the door of the phone box. Leslie! I slammed the receiver down. 'What are you doing in there?' he shouted.

'Ringing Louise,' I said, as I came out.

'Oh.'

'She's busy.'

'I'm off to the Wimpy bar. Coming?'

I walked along with him, feeling like a prisoner. Not one being led to his execution, but as if I was condemned to a life-sentence. Locked in a cell and left to rot.

Half an hour later I found I couldn't remember the phone number.

Three: The Fairground Summer

And when I had a chance to look for it again, the magazines had gone. Leslie's mother had put them out for the dustman. So that was that.

That was that: full stop. For months everything had grey edges. Other people, Leslie for example, went on living, developing, growing. I marked time. Or beat time, as in music, aware of hours, minutes, seconds even, that passed without anything happening. Locked in a cell and left to rot. No employment: I tried, but there was nothing. At night, watching the telly with Mum and Dad. Or drinking coffee at the Wimpy bar. Or going out with Louise: I wondered why she bothered to put up with me. Seeing Leslie occasionally. As I'd thought, he'd less time for me since he had broken the girl barrier. But things were more tolerable, curiously, during the winter when the rest of the world seemed dead as well, when frost and freezing wind shrivelled existence — plant, animal, human — back down inside itself, nipped the tendrils of growth; but in spring, in the first mild warm days when life stirred, I found depression at its most acute: other creatures revived, but not me. I was still withered. Dying inside myself, as a plant may do yet appear to be healthy, and only when it keels over does one notice putrescence has reached the outside leaves.

Yes, I know it's all very self-pitying. The old crude message on

urinal walls says your future is in your hands. True. Very true. But I hadn't the guts, the experience, the know-how, the confidence, the...anything. My ego had apparently been destroyed. Or, at least, severely damaged. I longed to talk to my parents. Who else? Up till now they had been the kind, patient listeners to all my troubles. Michael Tanner punched me on the nose; Roger Barnett stole my sweets; I dropped 10p and it rolled down a drain; I fell off my bike and grazed my knee and it hurts...
All the traumas of childhood they had soothed and mended, and when they couldn't do so they had consoled and calmed. This...impossible. I wrote letters in my head, telling them everything. I never actually put pen to paper. But why didn't I get in touch with that counselling organisation? Leslie banging on the phone-box door was hardly a good reason for not trying again. I could have found the number by ringing directory enquiries. So why didn't I? Cowardice. Not ready for it: it might be the start of a very long road leading God knows where, and I wasn't old enough, not sure enough of myself, to risk travelling on it.

> *Dear Mum and Dad,*
>> *By the time you've read this you'll know I'm homosexual.*

What on earth would I say after that bombshell? That I hoped one day to meet a boy and fall in love with him, live with him perhaps? How easy it would be for Leslie to say to his mother, 'I've met a really nice girl!' I could see in my mind's eye Mrs Radford welcoming her into the house. 'So you're Anne (or Julia or whatever her name was). I've heard so much about you!' My mum and my boy-friend? Huh! What could I write in a letter concerning my own gay life? That Leslie and I had had sex a score of times? Which would sound less shocking, that I'd thoroughly enjoyed every moment of it because I fancied him — or that he'd just needed a helping hand but no girl would volunteer hers? They'd say 'Get out of our house and never darken our doors again!' Yet we were the same two boys as the sweet innocent kids they'd always known and loved. The *same*, for God's sake! No better or worse than we'd ever been. We hadn't become villainous monsters, depraved moral outcasts.

Why don't parents listen to their children? They don't. Perhaps it's because they can't guess at where we've reached. The next stage always surprises them. And alarms them, because every move means one more knot in the string of dependence is loosened. If I told them I was gay, they wouldn't believe I was capable of knowing that I was; they'd think I was far too young to have realised such a thing about myself. Or that I was deliberately trying to hurt them, or shake them up for some selfish reason. Or that I was being trendy; a new fashion, like deciding to be a skinhead or a punk. They wouldn't have any idea of the hurt and pain that their attitude would be causing *me*. I imagined myself years ahead, coming home for a weekend, alone of course because I wouldn't be able to take a lover of my own sex into my parents' house: would the conversation turn to *my* life? Would my boy-friend's name even be mentioned? No. So whoever I could approach if I was in trouble, it would not be my parents.

Better, then, not to say anything. Better not to risk anything. Life would be easier that way. I thought.

That's why I didn't contact Parents' Enquiry, why I went round feeling dead inside. It seemed preferable.

Summer had one obvious compensation: I was still unemployed so I had all the time I could want in the sea. In the macho all-male world of the surf-board I was as good as anybody else, and I appeared to be no different from anybody else. As real a male as the next guy. Another attraction was that Leslie was no better than me; we were equals, and rivals. Once again, we spent hours together. We resumed our old routine of jogging before breakfast and weight-lifting at the gym. I looked at myself one night in the bathroom mirror and thought, you look pretty good, Ewan. Suntanned and fit. The muscles in my arms and chest had developed. A good curve to the biceps. Flat stomach. Even if I felt that inside I was of an inferior species, I could pass myself off as one of the real people. It was a bit like blacks painting their skins white and dying their curls blond, but that was not how I regarded it then.

Soon after our seventeenth birthdays a travelling fair came to town. Leslie went dotty over Kay, who worked on one of the hooplas. A good-looking girl, I suppose, with green eyes and long red hair, rather like Linda: funny how some people, once a pattern is set, fall for the same types, again and again. Kay had an effect on Leslie different from that of any other girl he had been involved with. He was in love for the first time in his life. He stopped coming to the beach, even though the surf was excellent. 'No girl is important enough to miss surfing,' I told him, but he was deaf to anything I said. The early-morning runs stopped. I hardly saw him at all, and when I did he was cool or off-hand.

· The Surf Club announced that it was holding a competition for juniors, with cash prizes. Leslie said he probably wouldn't enter for it; he was thinking of leaving Bude to find work. I was astonished. And upset; half the fun of the competition would be lost if he wasn't there. I could beat the other kids, I reckoned: Leslie was the only real challenge and I didn't want to come first merely because he wasn't available. I wanted to beat him for the prize. 'It simplifies things if I don't enter,' he said. 'Makes you the obvious favourite. You ought to be pleased.'

'Well, I'm *not* pleased.'

'Why? Are you jealous or something?'

'If you think I fancy your girl-friend, you couldn't be more wrong.'

'I didn't mean in that sense.'

'What did you mean, then?'

He wouldn't say, but I guessed he knew I felt sore about being dislodged as the number one person in his life. Kay persuaded him to enter for the competition, but that, surprisingly, didn't help my mood. When I nearly got drowned one morning after attempting a huge wave in an extremely rough sea, and had to be dragged out, frightened, choking, and unable to walk, I was even more upset. Some of the adult surfers told me off for being so reckless, and Leslie and Kay had to help me get dressed I felt so feeble. A few nights later we went to a disco and I was very rude to

Leslie. I was a bit drunk. When the fair left town, I tried to apologise and pick up the pieces but things weren't the same. I gathered from what he said that they'd made love, properly, the real thing: his first time. But he was depressed and unhappy, though it wasn't just that Kay was no longer there; something had happened that had humiliated him badly. When I asked him what it was he told me to sod off. Perhaps he'd had some silly idea about working with the fairground people so that his beautiful romance could continue, and they had refused to let him.

Our mothers went up to London; a women's club outing which meant they were away for a couple of nights. After they'd gone I left Dad asleep in front of the telly and went next door with some cans of beer. Leslie was bored, having nothing in particular to do, but not even the sight of alcohol made him pleased to see me. 'Don't you ever knock?' he said, as I came in.

But he opened one of the cans and drank from it, then switched on the television, pretending to find it totally absorbing.

I needed to talk, to move the situation between us back to what it had been before the fair came to town. But how? I wanted to say something about friendship, that what could exist between one boy and another had areas that no girl-friend could entirely replace. Without betraying myself, of course. It wasn't easy to know where to start, and my first words were clumsy, almost gave the game away. 'I can't see much difference when you think it all out,' I said, 'between having a girl-friend and going around with another boy.'

It was the first time since I'd arrived with the beer that he'd taken any real notice of me. 'I can think of a few pretty obvious differences,' he answered. 'What's the matter with you? Are you on the turn?'

Well, at least I had his attention. 'Don't be daft. What I meant was I'd rather talk to boys. To you . . . I never seem to have much to say when I'm with a girl. I get tongue-tied; I don't feel at ease. And they giggle so much, particularly when they're in a group. I sometimes think perhaps I'm . . . frightened of them.' Had I gone too far? Revealed too much? It wasn't altogether true, either: I was usually quite happy in Louise's company. 'Do you know what

40

I mean?' I asked.

'No.'

'So you prefer the company of girls.'

'*A* girl,' he said. 'I certainly wouldn't want to be the only male in a great gaggle of women. But *a* girl, one special person . . . of course it's more interesting than going around with people of your own sex all the time!'

'Well, I haven't found it so. I prefer your company to that of anybody else I know.'

'Don't you get bored, always knocking about with me?'

'Quite the opposite. I really enjoy being with you . . . doing things, surfing.'

'I want . . . out! No more Bude! I want the big bad world outside!' This wasn't getting us anywhere. It was yet another stage of life he was after now, one which excluded me completely: friendship, at the moment, was of no importance. 'I find girls fascinating,' he said. 'And I'm not thinking of the excitement of getting your hand inside a bra; I mean the way their minds work, their feelings. Everything about them.' He'd like to be married, he said; have a couple of kids: why not? 'It could be bloody marvellous!'

'When your friends get married . . . no, I mean when they get deeply involved . . . you lose them.' I looked straight at him. 'Like you and Kay.'

'You didn't like me being with Kay because you felt left out; is that what you're trying to tell me? You missed my company?'

'Yes.'

'Sometimes I think you're bloody pathetic, Ewan.'

'What do you mean?'

'You're asking me to stop doing what I want to do. Who do you think you are? If she walked through that door at this minute I wouldn't have any hesitation in telling you to fuck off! And if she was here all the time, living in Bude, you wouldn't see me for dust! What's the matter with you?'

'Nothing!'

'Well, shut up then and let me watch the television.'

'I was only trying to be friendly! Bringing you booze and

thinking you'd be fed up on your own with nothing to do.'

'I'm grateful for the beer. But I'm not fed up with being on my own.'

'I'll go if you like.' I *was* being pathetic; he was quite right. Somehow I'd lost control of this conversation; every time I opened my mouth I was making it all much worse.

'Do what you want,' he said. 'I couldn't care less.' I went to the door and hurried out, but he followed, shouting, 'Come here! I didn't mean it!' I should have gone straight home, keeping one last shred of dignity; to do anything else was cheap. But I had already stopped. I turned and walked slowly back into his house.

We watched the television. Or rather he did; I saw it but nothing registered. After about an hour he switched it off, came over to where I was sitting and touched me between the legs. 'I'm ... so randy anyone would do,' he said, rather glumly.

It was the last time it ever happened.

'*Are* you queer, Ewan?'

The moment I had been dreading for months. I licked my lips: my tongue suddenly felt dry. 'I have ... wondered,' I said. 'Occasionally.' My voice sounded high and strangulated.

'Seems to me you could be.'

'What about you?'

'Me?' He burst into laughter. '*Me*? You've got to be joking! Do you really think that's possible? I should hope you know me better than that!'

'Then ... I guess you're not.'

'It was just the two of us having a wank.'

'Yes.' A vile word to describe what I thought was something beautiful.

'Tell me ... do you fancy me?'

'Not in the slightest.'

'Thank God for that!' He smiled, apologetically. 'I wouldn't be able to stand that! I'd say, get out of my life. And I don't want to do such a thing, not to my best friend.'

'Am I?'

He nodded.

I went round there next morning, hoping he'd be up and ready for an early-morning run. There was no answer to my knock, but when I pushed at the door I found it unbolted. He was still in bed, fast asleep. My best friend. *He'd* said so! At that moment, I felt, despite everything, that I actually loved him. I was prepared to admit to myself I could make such a dangerous leap in the dark; but another part of me said don't be a *total* idiot: that way lies complete ruin. So I swallowed the feeling. Which wasn't a selfish emotion, not desire for sexual gratification. It was as if I could give him my entire being: stay with him in sickness and in health, defend him against any pain the world could ever stab him with. Make him happy. Whole.

I kissed him. On the mouth, very gently, so that he wouldn't open his eyes and be disgusted. A gift, love, worth more than all Arabia's oil. And I went downstairs and cooked his breakfast, feeling so light and joyous I wondered why I didn't float in space like an astronaut.

It was a disastrous blunder. If at the time I'd been able to think properly, I would have known before I started; but it's impossible to live a one-hundred-per-cent lie and keep your wits about you during every second of your existence. When the food was ready I went up to his bedroom. He was still asleep. Or so I thought. I pulled the quilt off: stark naked, with a massive erection. 'Caught right in the act!' I said. 'Hands off!'

He opened his eyes. 'How the hell did you get in here?'

'You forgot to lock the back door last night. *And* you forgot to put the cat out. What will your mother say? Oh, yes. Prize every time for size!' ('Prize every time for children' was what Kay shouted from her stall at the fair.) 'And remember that it makes you blind!'

He leapt out of bed, extremely angry. And punched me hard on the mouth. Blood on my lips. 'Get out of here and stay out!' he yelled. 'Bloody stupid fool!!'

I sagged against the wall. 'I've cooked your breakfast for you. It's on the table.'

'Who asked you to run round and do my jobs for me? I'm quite capable of making my own breakfast. *Get out*!!'

I turned tail and fled. This time I was not called back.

I deserved it, I suppose. Well, not deserved it, except in the sense that I'd walked straight into a situation — had been doing so for months — that could only end up like this. People being what they are. Selfish and frightened and threatened and nasty and...human. I kept away from him, avoided him at all costs. On the beach I helped Phil Cloke with life-saving practices. He was one of the guys who'd bawled me out when I nearly got myself drowned. It was interesting and useful, and in the sea I was still a real man in the eyes of the others: butch, heterosexual.

It was the afternoon of the surfing championship. Chilly late June weather. After Kay had left there was no more talk from Leslie about not competing. I was glad, and determined to come first; it would be a sweet revenge. Show him that I didn't have to screw women to win this most male of sporting events. I hadn't seen him for a week, and when I did, in the Surf Club changing-room, I walked right past without recognising him. But something familiar made me turn round: he had permed his hair.

'What do you reckon?' he asked, grinning.

'You look like a poodle!'

We came first in our heats, and as I surveyed the opposition in the final I knew it was between him and me. Our fifth and last wave was superb, the biggest of the day, a real giant that rose up and up: it demanded we went in the tube, the most difficult of all surfing manoeuvres. I was terrified it would disintegrate on top of me before I could shoot sideways along the slope of it, but there was no time for thought or hesitation: I simply did it. Success! Marvellous!

Leslie had done it too. We stood on the sand, laughing and smiling at each other, then hugged like footballers when the winning goal has just been kicked into the net.

We were placed first equal.

I was thrilled: ideas of petty revenge seemed far away; we were joint champions! Justice had been done. 'It's the first time anything good has ever happened to me!' I cried.

'A fair result,' was his comment. 'A very fair result.'

In the showers at the Surf Club, I said 'I'm sorry about the other morning.'

'There's nothing to be sorry about. I was the one who lost his temper.'

It sounded less than warm. I did not answer for a while, but soaped myself all over. I watched him and he watched me. He knew. Knew what I was. That I fancied him like mad. 'We're growing apart,' I said.

'Yes.'

'Or to be more accurate, *you're* growing apart.'

'Yes. I want a job. I want a girl. Above all, I want to leave Bude.'

'I shall miss you. A lot.'

He walked away and sat on a bench. Then covered himself with a towel.

'I'm leaving on a jet plane,' I sang. 'Don't know when I'll be back again; oh babe, I have to go.'

When he was dressed he said 'See you around.' And left.

Next day he hitch-hiked to Newquay, and found himself a job in the still-room of a hotel. At the end of the season he went to London and worked as a builder's labourer. I didn't see him again till Christmas. Every night, for weeks, he was in my mind's eye as I tossed myself off in bed.

Mum's fortieth birthday. It seemed incredibly old to me, though I had a vague suspicion that she was more hide-bound by routine, more a creature of habit, than many people of her age. Leslie's mother was born in the same year, but she was much more inclined to do things on impulse: the previous week she had been dancing at a night club in Exeter till two in the morning. I've never seen my mother dance anywhere, let alone at a night club. Forty: born in nineteen thirty-eight, a wartime upbringing. Mum had often told me about evacuees and doodlebugs, what Plymouth looked like after the destruction and Exeter with its heart ripped out.

I gave her a dozen mugs, each one different: those we used for tea and coffee were so old and chipped and stained they should have been thrown out years ago. It cost me most of a week's dole money, but that didn't matter. In Bude the only things to spend money on were alcohol and fags. And she liked the present. Very much.

We went out to dinner to celebrate, an almost unheard-of event in our family. It had only happened once before, and that was so long ago I can't remember why we did. Before I dressed, in a clean pair of jeans and a blue shirt, I surveyed myself in the mirror once again. (It had become a habit; I don't know why: I don't think I'm all that worried about my appearance. At least, no more than anybody else.) Seventeen. Still thin. A hairless chest: I don't suppose that will ever change. But I shaved every other day now. And that thing down there, my cock, not exactly invisible. More than ready for active service. The outside of me was all right: and no one could see the horrible mess inside.

It was a good evening, with Mum and Dad determined to enjoy themselves. Our family at its best. Though Dad looked weird in a jacket and tie.

'It's choking me,' he said, fingering his collar. 'Perhaps it's shrunk in the wash.'

Mum laughed. 'You're putting on weight; that's all. Have a good look at yourself in the bathroom mirror some time.'

'I'd rather look at you any day of the week.' He squeezed her hand.

'Or page three of the *Sun*.'

'No. Not really. There's nothing in the paper that's a patch on my wife.'

She seemed pleased, and embarrassed, and giggled like Adrienne and Karen in the Wimpy bar. 'Everything all right, Ewan?' she asked.

'Yes. I'm trying to visualise you two when you were my age.'

'Is it difficult?'

'A little.' I sipped my wine. Sauternes: far too sweet for my taste, but it was Mum's favourite.

'We didn't know each other when we were your age,' Dad said, as he tucked into steak, chips and tomatoes. What a peculiar meal to order, I thought, when you go out to dinner for the first time in ten years! He could have steak, chips and tomatoes any day of the week at home. And did, when we could afford to buy the steak. I thought it a splendid opportunity to eat something I'd never had before, and I'd decided on chicken chasseur, which was proving to be quite delicious.

'We met when I was nineteen,' Mum said. 'At a dance. I was working behind that same baker's counter even then! If I'd known I'd still be there twenty-one years on I'd have died on the spot!'

'Eighteen,' Dad corrected. 'You were eighteen.'

'No. You're thinking of some other girl.'

He grinned. 'Could be! But I gave all that up when I met you. When you find the right one, then all that playing around seems an absolute waste of time.'

'If she *is* the right one.'

'Come off it! I think we love each other now more than we ever did then. Though it was pretty good at the time, I remember.'

'You grow into one another.'

He nodded. 'Yes. Marvellous, isn't it?'

'We ought to do this more often. Come out and enjoy ourselves.'

'Question of money.'

'I know.'

I couldn't make up my mind whether I was watching something that was perfect: or was it a horrible kind of trap, a total delusion? Narrow, boring, restricted; the little square inch most people allowed themselves, and because it was just like everybody else's lives you kidded yourself it was the ultimate pinnacle of happiness? It certainly wasn't going to be my life. But whether that was a good thing or not I didn't know.

'You'll be in the same position one day, Ewan,' Dad said. 'And we'll have grandchildren to look forward to.'

'Give him a chance!' Mum protested.

'Oh, he'll have plenty of chances. More than we had, I daresay. Don't you want grandchildren?'

'Oh yes! All the pleasures of babies without any of the responsibilities.'

'Suppose I never get married,' I said.

'I hope you do,' Mum said. 'Life can be very lonely if you don't.'

'Till death do us part is an insurance policy against being lonely, is it?'

'Well...you don't think that at the time, of course.'

'I certainly didn't,' Dad said.

'Lots of people don't get married these days,' I pointed out. 'And it isn't like it used to be, being left on the shelf, I mean. Lots of people don't *choose* to get married.'

'One of the reasons why the world's in such a terrible mess.' Mum was never a very logical person.

'All boys of your age think like that,' Dad said. 'He always wants it without taking her to the altar; she wants the ceremony first. The old, old story. I was exactly the same at seventeen. But you get caught in the end.'

'Caught?'

'I don't mean in that sense, though plenty are. If we had been, you'd be several years older! No...I mean walking up the aisle and all that sort of caper.'

I didn't reply; the subject wasn't worth pursuing. It was like trains on parallel lines; the chance of meeting was non-existent. As I said before, parents don't hear you. Don't ever wonder who you really are: they assume you're a carbon copy of them, and, if you actually show them that you aren't, they get very disturbed. And I didn't want to disturb my parents. Particularly when they were enjoying themselves.

'Ah...this is nice!' Dad said when we were back home, and he was sitting in his favourite armchair, tie off now and collar loosened, a cup of tea in front of him. 'Did you have a good time, Ewan?'

'Yes. I did.'

'I'm glad. It wouldn't have been the same without you, you know.'

'That's very true,' Mum said.

Four: First Love

The time after Leslie went was bleak and empty. The weather was beautiful and the surf good: I took my board into the sea every day, and I liked the other kids looking up to me now I'd won a competition, even if I'd had to share first prize with somebody else. But I was lonely as hell. I thought about Leslie non-stop: working, even if the job might prove boring and badly paid, and away from home and able to spend all his free hours with girls he'd met. He had shifted so easily into the next stage of life: and I was still in Bude, out of work, and alone.

But two important things happened that summer. I'd more or less given up going around with the gang: I hadn't been in the Wimpy bar for weeks. I just couldn't continue having the same old conversations with Alan and Little Michael about tits and how far you could go with Molly or Juicy Lucy. I couldn't relax, pretending to be fascinated with something that didn't interest me in the least. But if I didn't join in, they'd ask questions; 'Are you on the turn?' Though I was probably more scared about what they might say behind my back than to my face. I avoided them all.

Then one morning I bumped into Louise. Quite literally bumped into her. I was rounding the corner by Mrs Radford's shop, my mind far away — in Newquay, I guess — and I banged her on the head with my surf-board, very hard.

Apologies, and 'Are you all right?' and 'I'm fine; it didn't really hurt' for several minutes, then she smiled and said 'Where've you been? Nobody's set eyes on you for weeks!'

'Busy,' I answered.

'Got a job, have you?'

'No.'

'Same as everyone else, then. Except for Wimpy John and Leslie, of course, and Adrienne. So what do you do all day?'

'Surf.'

'You think more of that board than any girl, I reckon.'

I laughed. 'Well...making the most of the good weather,' I said. 'Soon be autumn.'

'Why don't you come round tonight? There's a good film at the Picture House. Or we could stay in; I've just got a couple of fabulous new records. Mum and Dad won't be there: darts at the Red Lion for him, and she's going to visit her brother in Stratton.'

I looked at her. All that horrible make-up. Knockers that left other boys' eyes hanging out on stalks. The thought of holding her in my arms and kissing her ... once it had vaguely interested me, but the idea of it now made me shudder. 'I don't know,' I mumbled. 'There's something I might have to do this evening.'

'Oh, come on!' she said. 'You can't bash me around the face with that thing in broad daylight *and* turn down an invitation. Half past seven?'

And before I could think of a good excuse, she'd hurried off.

How the hell did you get yourself into this mess? I asked the reflection in the mirror that evening. I could, I supposed, simply not go. Or...I could regard it as a final test of whether I really was gay or not. Not very fair on her, though. Shit! *She* asked *me.* It was an extremely hot night. Sticky, heavy, with a promise of thunder. I was wearing only a shirt and jeans: but even with as little as that I was sweating like a pig. Nerves, possibly. My stomach felt knotted, and I couldn't eat much tea. My mother raised an eyebrow and looked amused, but she didn't say anything till I was leaving. I told her I wasn't sure when I'd be back and she said 'Don't have too good a time,' which made me blush scarlet and feel like an absolute idiot.

A bloody awful time it proved to be, but some of it was surprising, and...in the long run, helpful. What was obvious, almost as soon as I got inside Louise's front door, was that she wanted to go a lot further than we'd done previously; another boy would have found he had only to tilt the situation slightly, and he might have everything he wanted. It was nothing she said; it was the way she looked and moved that told me, the sense she managed to convey of a barely concealed excitement. We danced to her new records and drank pints of ice-cold orange juice. Then danced again, and I was kissing her because she'd be upset if I didn't. Her hands were under my shirt, and, yes, it did excite me; then we were on the sofa and I had her bra undone so quickly that even Leslie would have envied the speed. Something down in my jeans stirred. But when I touched her, and felt hair and sticky damp, I went completely limp.

I looked at her, and, suddenly, I felt quite disgusted. There was no hope of an erection now. I shut my eyes and tried to imagine her hands were Leslie's. He only had to touch my penis and it flipped vertical.

'What's wrong?' she asked. She sounded a bit annoyed: I suppose it was a kind of metaphorical slap in the face.

'I don't know.' I opened my eyes.

'It doesn't matter, Ewan.' Her voice was softer, concerned.

I zipped up my jeans, and buttoned my shirt. I couldn't stand, any longer, her seeing me half naked. 'It matters a hell of a lot!'

'It isn't just me, is it? I . . . think I know.'

'Know what?'

She stood up, re-arranging her clothes. She shook her head, smiling a little sadly. 'You don't have to say; it isn't necessary. Shall I make some coffee?'

I just wanted to get out of the house and leave this dreadful scene as far behind me as I possibly could; I wanted to walk on the cliffs, do something violently physical, and think and think and *think*. But I said 'All right' and she went into the kitchen. I sat on the sofa, puffing and choking on a cigarette. It soothes the nerves, people say. What rubbish! I ground it out, half finished.

Had she told the other girls? Linda, Juicy Lucy, Adrienne? Were they, even at this moment, sniggering about it? Louise knew! I'd always thought her nice but not exceptionally intelligent: yet she had guessed. How could that be? I didn't look effeminate, a prancing fairy, some drag act. Maybe it didn't need intelligence, not that sort of intelligence. Intuition, sympathy,

51

awareness of other people: Louise had all those qualities. She was warm and kind-hearted. I'd been so wrapped up in my own problems I'd almost forgotten what she was really like.

I followed her into the kitchen. She was singing, that old Simon and Garfunkel number 'A time it was, and what a time it was, it was ... a time of innocence ... and confidences.' It sounded really sad. And horribly true. She looked up and smiled. 'It's just ready. I've put two sugars in yours. Do you want a biscuit?'

I sat down, buried my head in my arms, and burst into tears. Slowly, ever so slowly, the tension drained out. I said 'I'd better explain.'

'Ewan, you don't have to!'

Nevertheless, I did. I told her everything. What I knew I was and how it scared me and that I didn't know what to do about it. What had happened with Leslie. She listened, saying yes and no in the right places. And she didn't mind! The relief that brought! More than her saying she'd kept her ideas to herself, hadn't even dropped a hint to the others. But I was pretty pleased about that, too. 'They haven't a clue,' she said, more than once. 'How could they? I guessed, only because we've ... well ... been out together.'

'It's been good, talking,' I said. 'You don't know how good!'

'Maybe you should have told me before.'

'Yes. Yes, I reckon so.'

'Your only answer is ... to find other people like yourself.'

I nodded. Though I wasn't ready for that. One day, but not yet. I was still too unhappy with being what I was, not reconciled to it at all.

'You're great!' I said. 'I wish I could appreciate it better!'

She laughed. 'I expect you'll do as you are. You'll have to, won't you?' I stood up and hugged her. Swung her round the room. 'Put me down!!' she screamed. I did, and discovered I was staring at her parents.

'What on earth is going on?' her mother asked.

I saw a lot of Louise during the next few weeks. We went to a disco one evening. The gang were all there: Louise and I smiled at each other several times, a look that said 'We know, but *they* don't.' And some afternoons we sat on the cliffs and talked. Then she started going out with a guy called Martin, and I didn't see so much of her. I began to keep a diary. When it rained I'd scribble away, more to prevent loneliness and boredom than for any other reason. Not the usual stuff people write in diaries, like 'One p.m. lunched at home' or '8.30 meet Louise,' but thoughts and feelings. It passed the time: there was nothing else to do. I went after jobs when I saw them advertised, but it was all hopeless. Nobody wanted a seventeen-year-old with four C.S.E.s, even though I had a grade one in English.

Then the other interesting event of that summer occurred: during the first week of September.

It was one of those magical days that seem to come only in September and early October, when the softness of the light makes everything precious and golden and the air is so still you think the world has stopped turning. Yet the shadows are long — shafts of slanting greyness — and you know the earth has been nudged a fraction towards winter. And distances are hazy; there is no edge to sea and sky. I took my board with me, but there was no chance of surfing: the sea was so calm you could scarcely hear it.

I wasn't going back into town on a day like this. I walked along the beach, beyond the holiday-makers enjoying the year's last moments of freedom: next week the schools re-opened and the sand would stay almost virgin till April. The board was a nuisance; I should have left it at the Club. However, I walked on. Past Northcott Mouth where ten summers ago Leslie and I had learned to swim, and round Menachurch Point, beyond which, if you look back, you've got rid of Bude, any hint that it exists. Ahead is Sandy Mouth, nearly a mile away; today it was a mile without people. Except for three men bouncing a beach ball.

I took off my jeans and shirt, then stretched out on my towel enjoying the sun on my skin. I wasn't far from the ball-game, but I didn't want to go too near; it would have looked odd. One of the men, slim and suntanned, with long dark hair parted in the middle and reaching down to his shoulders, was very attractive. Londoners, I guessed from their voices. Eventually the game stopped and they lay on the sand. Then two of them stood up; they seemed to be leaving, though I couldn't hear the conversation. There was a lot of joking and laughter; the dark-haired one didn't want to go for some reason, and the others found this very funny. They walked off in the direction of Sandy Mouth. The man who was left turned over and looked at me.

I decided to go for a swim. As I went past him, he smiled and said 'Hi.'

I stopped. I felt, suddenly, very tense: that knotted-up sensation in the stomach again. 'Hi,' I answered.

'I think I'll join you,' he said. He had a chain round his neck, on it a flashy silver pendant. He was very hairy. From his throat down to where it disappeared inside his shorts.

We ran into the sea. It was warm, and almost as flat as a swimming pool, only a hint of rise and fall. 'You swim well,' he said, then dived and grabbed at my legs, pulling me under. I surfaced, shook the water from my eyes, and grinned. 'What's your name?' he asked.

'Ewan.'

'I'm Paul. The others are Jay and Derek. Del for short. We're on holiday, renting a cottage in Coombe Valley.'

'I live here,' I said. 'In Bude, that is.'

He made a face. 'Don't like Bude.'

'It's a dump.'

'Come on. Let's sunbathe.' We walked up the beach. 'Bring your things over here,' he said. I did so, wondering why I was obeying the commands of a total stranger so easily.

We talked for a long time. He had just completed his probationary year as a teacher, at Deptford in south-east London. He was twenty-three. A surf enthusiast, but, he said ruefully, he'd obviously chosen the wrong week. I told him about sharing first prize in the competition. 'We're just amateurs,' he said, 'me and Del and Jay. If we get a fortnight each year in the sea, we're lucky.' The conversation drifted on, technical stuff: types of wave, different equipment, the personalities in the England team. How nice it would be to practise in Hawaii. But certain things in the talk seemed odd: half-finished statements he left hanging in the air, as if he wanted me to pick them up and work them out for myself, or maybe throw him back something of a similar nature. 'Del and Jay are together,' he said. Then gazing at me, a wide smile on his face, 'I'm just looking. Looking around, that is'. But I didn't know what the answers were that he expected, so I said nothing. He had green eyes: open, trusting. Green as wet grass. There were some long silences. After one of them, he asked 'Do you have a girl-friend?'

'No.'

'Between girls, is it?'

'No. Not really.'

Another silence. 'Maybe it's a boy you're interested in.' I shut my eyes. 'Or maybe you aren't sure yet.' He rolled over, his hand brushing my leg. He didn't take it away. The effect was the same as Leslie touching me. 'Perhaps I should go,' he said, laughing. 'I don't want to be accused of corrupting the young.'

I opened my eyes and sat up. 'Don't go! Please don't go!'

He said, very quietly, 'You're beautiful.' And he kissed me. The first time in my life I had been kissed by someone of my own sex. 'Is it safe here?' he asked.

'Safe for what?'

'Oh, Ewan! You *are* young and inexperienced!'

'Yes, I am.' I looked round. There was no one in sight. And he was touching my skin, caressing me, sucking my cock, arousing me so much that I felt there could be no stopping now even if coach-loads of people suddenly appeared on top of the cliffs. It wasn't a bit like it had been with Leslie. This was making love: so much feeling passing between us, so much gentleness. We came at exactly the same moment, in each other's hands.

'I think, somehow, you needed that,' he said.

'I did! Christ, oh, I did! You just don't know! My first time. My first proper time, that is. I feel . . . oh, I can't explain! Terrified.'

'Terrified?'

'I don't want to be gay! Suppose people find out? And how can you ever be happy?'

'Aren't you happy at this moment?'

'Yes. Yes!' I stood up, ran down the beach, then jumped in the air and shouted at the top of my voice 'I am *happy*!!' When I returned, Paul was roaring with laughter. 'What's the matter?'

55

'I think you forgot you've no clothes on!'

I looked at myself and grinned. 'Yes! I did!'

I sat on my towel. 'There isn't anything wrong with being gay,' he said. 'When you're sure enough of yourself to realise that it doesn't matter if people know, you'll value the ones who accept it and not give a damn for the others who don't or won't or can't. It's true there can be a lot of problems, a lot more than if you're straight. But that's not so important as being content to be what you are. That's the most difficult thing to learn...to love yourself. Much more difficult for people like you and me because of what society thinks of us. But you've as much right to be here as any other person, with as much right to find partners of your own sex as they have to find the opposite. And as for being happy, provided you're glad to be Ewan, you have the same chances as the rest of the human race. Just like the boy next door who screws a different girl every night. Or the one who's faithful to his wife and two-point-four kids and mortgage. The *same* chance.'

'Ah...the boy next door!' I told him all about Leslie.

'Perhaps he's bisexual. And won't come to terms with it.' He thought for a moment. 'Your mate's not done you much good, has he? In fact, I reckon he's done you a lot of positive harm. Without intending to, of course.'

'What do you mean?'

'He's landed you with a huge inferiority complex. Because he's so attractive and sexy and the girls wet their knickers when they see him, and he's left home and found himself a job, he's made you feel you're still a snotty-nosed kid. You're even jealous that he has an outsize cock. As if that added one iota of difference to the total sum of human happiness! What's wrong with your own, for God's sake? You certainly know what to do with it! You've ended up more unsure of yourself than you were in the first place.' It was absolutely true. But it didn't stop me being envious of Leslie, wishing I was him. Not one bit. 'The worst thing you did was to let him have sex with you. Oh yes, I know that's easily said. But it's caused more heartache than happiness, hasn't it? I should give him up if I were you. Not see him again.'

'I couldn't do that!'

He shrugged his shoulders. 'Perhaps you're in love with him.'

'No. I've wondered if I was, but . . . I don't think so. He isn't at all lovable. Not like you.' I wished I hadn't said that, the moment the words were out of my mouth. 'What a stupid thing to say!' I muttered, reddening to the roots of my hair.

'It was a sweet thing to say.' He touched my face, then stood up and started to dress. Jeans. Lemon yellow tee-shirt. 'I have to go now. The others will be wondering where the hell I am.'

'When they went . . . why were they laughing so much?'

'You don't know?'

'Because they knew you fancied me, and you said you wanted to try your luck?'

He put his feet in his sandals, and smiled. 'You're not that green, then! Look . . . would you like to come to the cottage with us?'

I glanced at my watch. There was plenty of time before I had to be home, but I shook my head. I needed to be by myself. To relive the day, and think: decide if I wanted to see him again. 'I have to get back,' I said.

'What about tonight?'

Decisions. I had to make them now. 'I'm not doing anything,' I said.

'Good. We usually go for a quiet drink in a country pub most evenings. The Bush at Morwenstow, or the Old Smithy at Welcombe. But you're the local lad; you know better than we do . . . you decide where.'

'What time?'

'About seven?' I nodded. 'We'll pick you up in the car at . . . Will the corner of Kilkhampton Street do?'

'Yes. But I have to be indoors at half past eleven or midnight.'

'Oh.' He seemed disappointed.

I smiled. 'I'm still a kid, Paul! With parents who don't like it if I'm in late and who want to know why. I'm the same age as one of your sixth-formers.'

He shuddered. 'Don't give me heart attacks!'

'See you at seven.'

The week that followed was an oasis in a desert. Afterwards, I thought nothing so marvellous would ever happen to me again; indeed, I wondered if I had just dreamed it all, spent seven days outside space and time, lost somewhere in a figment of my imagination. But no, it *was* real, and the ending a particularly cruel piece of real life. I should have seen that coming, but I had no experience to guide me. The cloudless September weather held — hot, still. We lay on the beach and walked along country lanes, and in the evenings we went to the cottage, then, later, to a pub. Jay and Del came with us in the car to Tintagel, another time to Clovelly. They had been an affair for nearly three years; had met at the university where Paul had also been a student, and they, too, were teachers in London schools. They were fun to be with: uncomplicated people, joking and laughing nearly all the time, and they also knew when to take themselves off and leave Paul and me on our own. I was head over heels in love. All the clichés: walking on air, strolling hand in hand into the sunset.

It was not, now, two boys masturbating, one of them imagining the other was a girl. Screwing. At first I was frightened; it would be painful, I thought. Did I really feel an urge for this? It was, perhaps, a denial of my maleness? I should penetrate: that was what it was for. Wasn't it? Everybody said so. Into Paul? The idea was ridiculous. I wanted him inside me; I wanted to be fucked. Only that would give me absolute satisfaction, emotionally.

'If it hurts,' he said, kissing me, stroking me with his fingers, 'I won't do it. I promise. This will make it easier'.

'What?'

'K.Y. A lubricant.'

Pain, yes, quite severe — he wasn't small — but only for a moment as he entered: after that, though it still hurt a bit (I would get used to that in time; indeed soon there was never any discomfort), it was the most natural, normal and utterly beautiful experience. His hand, still slippery with K.Y., on my cock, a sensation more superb than any I had ever felt, then orgasm so perfect I thought I was changed from a body into pure dazzling light. And he, coming, the spurt and gasp of him inside me: oh, yes; this is what life is for, Ewan: for this I was made.

Kisses, gentle hands touching skin. Drifting towards sleep.

'I don't have to wonder if you enjoyed it,' he said, later. I smiled. No answer was needed. 'Or if we were the right way round.'

I opened my eyes. 'I just want it again. For ever and ever like that. Till I'm ninety-six and dying.'

I hardly saw my parents; in for a meal, then out again. It didn't matter being absent during the day; with both Mum and Dad at work, there was no one to ask what I was up to. But they looked at me quizzically at tea-time, or when I returned at midnight. They said nothing, but clearly they knew something was afoot. What they thought that something was emerged when I asked Mum if I could stay over at Bookworm John's; he was giving a party, I said. (This was a lie, an elaborate invention so that I could, just once, sleep with Paul for the whole night. I felt bad; I wasn't in the habit of deceiving my parents: at least, not over big things like that.)

'I don't know,' she said.

'Why ever not?' I was surprised; I'd stayed at John's before. And Alan's and Leslie's.

She looked hard at me. 'Are you sure it's John you'll be staying with?'

'Of course!' It was dreadful! My face would certainly tell her I was lying.

'We've scarcely seen you all week. This house has turned into the Macrae Hotel, I reckon.' She smiled. 'I hadn't realised you and Louise were so close.'

'Louise!'

'Oh. It isn't her, then?' I didn't answer. 'Of course it's Louise! You can't pull the wool over my eyes!' She laughed. 'She's a nice girl. I'm glad. But . . . I don't want you getting yourself into a situation where you'll both end up doing something you'll regret. And staying out all night . . . could . . .'

I had a sudden wild impulse to tell her the truth, but I quickly repressed it. I stared at her, and said, eventually, 'I'm seventeen. *Not* a kid any longer.' I left the room, and hurried out of the house, in case the conversation became even more embarrassing. Later, Paul and I laughed about it; but my laughter covered up sadness. A gay existence meant lie after lie would have to be told, particularly to my parents. The gulf between me and them suddenly seemed a vast chasm. I'd have to be two people, one for home, one for away. It was tragic. Hateful and wicked! I began to feel as I had when I first realised — there was something loathsome about me.

Friday: tomorrow Paul would be going back to London. I couldn't bear the thought of it. Nothing had been said about seeing each other again; he hadn't suggested I came and stayed with him. I didn't even know his address and phone number. 'I wish I could come with you,' I said.

'It isn't possible.'

'Why not? What's to hold me in Bude? I haven't got a job. Maybe I could get one in London. Paul . . . please . . . why not?'

He shook his head. 'It wouldn't do.'

'I don't understand.'

'Do you really think it would work? You told me yourself you were the same age as one of my sixth-formers. Pupil and teacher living together . . . that would involve some careful planning, wouldn't it?'

'I'm not your pupil.'

'But I'm the first person you've ever fallen for, the first you've had any real sex with . . . the first . . . everything! To run away from home, to live with me, it would be . . . disastrous! You need much more experience, much more life, before you can make decisions like that. If you met me again in a few years' time, it might be very different.'

'You sod.'

'Yes, it sounds like that, doesn't it! But you know, deep down, I'm right.' I did know it, yes, but I didn't want it spelled out. 'You're sweet, Ewan, and fun . . . and beautiful. As a person, I mean, not just a body. I can't say "I love you." I couldn't say it to anyone, after only a week. Though I could be more than half *in* love.'

Later, over coffee with Jay and Del in the kitchen, when they were discussing what time they ought to leave in the morning, I said again, 'I want to come with you.'

There was a long silence, then Jay said, rather sharply, 'You haven't told him. That's not nice, Paul. I don't like you for that.'

'Told me what?'

'Paul has a boy-friend — Steve. They live together; they share a flat. Steve is away in America; he's been there nearly four months.'

'So what does that make me?' Paul said angrily. 'A monster? A bloody monster? Does it? Don't come the holier-than-thou bit, Jason!'

'I'm not! I wouldn't! Del and I aren't always faithful. What people of our age are when their lover's away for four months? I'm not condemning you for that! But you should have told Ewan. At least you could have been honest!'

'Stop it!' I shouted. 'I don't want to hear!'

'How *could* I tell him?' Paul said. 'I wanted to. I tried . . . but it stuck in my throat. He's never met anyone else . . . He thinks the sun shines out of my arse. It was beautiful. And now it's ruined.' He buried his face in his hands. 'I didn't want to hurt him!'

'You *have* hurt him,' Jay said.

'*You* have! *You* have!'

'He had to know!'

'It's not ruined,' Del said. He was speaking to me: it was the first time in this conversation anyone had thought me worth including. Paul and Jay had been arguing as if I wasn't in the room. 'And it's still beautiful,' he added.

'I'm sorry, Ewan,' Paul said. 'I'm so sorry!'

'It's all right,' I answered, trying to put on a brave face. 'I still love you.'

But it certainly hurt. As much as the fact that he wasn't there any longer. The days were an aching, yawning, lonely emptiness. The weather broke, and there was no more surfing. And no jobs, anywhere. I spent a lot of time writing in my diary. I'd been duped: it had been just another bloody holiday romance. September, October, November. I felt almost suicidal at times. Then, just after Christmas, I experienced another shattering blow.

Five: The Diary

I kept my diary in a record case — my only possession that had a lock and key. There it stayed, between two albums, Deep Purple and Pink Floyd. My parents would never find it there. One evening I forgot: I left it where I'd been reading it, on my bed, and went out to see Louise.

'We found this,' my mother said, holding it up, when I came in.

My heart nearly turned over. 'And you read it?'

'Yes.' Her voice trembled. My father sat on the sofa, looking utterly bewildered.

After a long silence during which they both stared at me, and I gazed at the floor, wishing I could die that instant or at least have a stroke or an epileptic fit, I said, quietly, 'You shouldn't have done that. You had no business.'

'I went to your room, just to put some clothes away,' my mother said. 'I saw it and picked it up, wondering what it was. That's all. It was open...September the fifth...' She began to cry.

'So you couldn't resist reading it from cover to cover.'

'You're taking the wrong attitude, Ewan,' my father said, heavily. He filled his pipe with elaborate slowness. 'We shouldn't have read it; that's true. You've as much right to your own privacy as we have, and that's a difficult thing for a parent to learn. But the fact is we have read it. We're extremely upset. Upset...the word's ridiculous! Your mother's beside herself.

Devastated!'

'And you?'

He didn't answer; just shook his head and made a helpless gesture with his hands. I stared at the clock on the mantelpiece, the Christmas cards, the blank television screen, and tried to concentrate, to hold on to these trivial props of everyday life as if they could prevent my whole world from drowning. The Christmas cards were the same as they had been a few hours ago; this room was the same. And I was engulfed in quicksand.

'I can't believe it,' my mother said, drying her eyes. 'I can't believe you're ... like that!' She couldn't bring herself to say any of the words that gave me a label. 'How could you be? We've brought you up as decently and honestly as we know how ... We must have done something wrong somewhere!' Her hands were shaking. 'I don't know what! I wish I did, then perhaps we could put it right ... It must be our fault!'

'It's not your fault,' my father said. 'It's not mine, either.' I was about to say it wasn't anyone's fault; I was like that and probably always had been. Maybe from birth. But he added 'There's always one rotten apple in any barrel.' The shock of those words was like having a bucket of cold water thrown in my face.

'Perhaps it's just those dreadful people you've met,' my mother went on. 'This ... Paul. He should be behind bars! Teaching children in a school! But ... how could you? And Leslie! I'd never have believed it!'

'Leslie is not homosexual,' I said.

'But he started you in these ... practices. And all this time I thought there was something between you and Louise ... When I thought you were out with her, you were doing ... How could you deceive us like that!' Her left eye had begun to blink uncontrollably, a nervous tic that always happened when she was in great stress. 'The lies, the deceit ... I just can't understand it!'

'I haven't deceived you. You merely assumed.'

'I want you to promise you won't ever see these people again ... Paul and the others ... and Leslie. Thank God he's not at home! What on earth would his mother say?'

Mrs Radford, I imagined, would be inclined to be more tolerant

63

than my parents. What she would think of me I didn't know, but, as far as Leslie was concerned, while she would not exactly approve of her son having sex with another boy, she'd probably regard it as something that happened occasionally in the maturing process: mildly reprehensible, but not the end of civilisation as we know it. And the girls in his life she'd feel were his business, not hers. We were, both of us, only a few months off eighteen, for God's sake! 'If you tell Mrs Radford,' I said, 'I'll never forgive you.'

'We've no intention of doing so,' my father said. 'It's you we're worried about. You're not homosexual! How could you be? It's impossible. You've come under all sorts of bad influences; that's what the trouble is. You just imagine you are. You're far too young to have any real ideas about it. I think . . . you ought to find some help.'

'Help?'

'Your mother says she'll have a word with Doctor Pearce. He might know someone.'

'I am not going to see a psychiatrist!' I said, very firmly. 'I am not!! I'll work out my own problems, thank you very much. I'm *not* mentally ill. I thought, oh, a year ago, that maybe I was . . . but I know now that I'm not!'

'I didn't say you were mentally ill,' my father said, patiently. 'Just extremely muddled. And you'll do what I tell you! You're my son; you live in this house, and you're not yet eighteen. I won't have you seeing this Paul again. You won't go out alone with Leslie. And you'll be back here by ten thirty at night. Those are orders!'

'If I refuse to obey?'

'You can get out. For good. You'll be no son of mine.'

Did he really mean what he said? I couldn't believe it. He was a loving, caring person. Or he had always seemed to be. I never went round thinking other dads were better than mine. And would I disobey him? I might deceive and lie perhaps, but I wouldn't openly rebel. Cowardice? Because I was afraid of him? Couldn't face the idea of being cast out into the world, absolutely alone and penniless, at the age of seventeen? Yes, partly. But more than that, I loved him. And Mum. I wanted the relationship I thought I'd always had with them to continue. How could I live with myself if they threw me out of the house?

'I'm not likely to see Paul,' I said. 'I don't know where he lives; I don't even know his phone number.'

'Well, that's something.'

'But you can't stop me seeing Leslie. I mean, how can you? I know he's not at home, but when he does come back, what then? Suppose he speaks to me over the fence? Do I ignore him? He's my mate, my best friend!'

'I didn't say you weren't to speak to him. I don't want you spending long periods of time together, that's all.'

'I wish we'd never set eyes on him!' my mother said.

'Mum, that's silly! I told you, he isn't gay. That happened ages ago.'

'Yes . . . and look what it's done to you!' She burst into tears. 'I wish you'd never been born! Oh God! I wish I was dead!'

My father moved to her, protectively. He looked at me, and said 'See what you've done?'

I ran out of the room and out of the house, slamming the front door. It was raining, and there was a chill wind. I had no coat, but I hardly felt how cold it was. I walked for miles, just hoping a car might drive carelessly round a corner, run over me and kill me. Eventually I found myself on the cliffs. The sea boiled and churned, tossing up columns of spray, dashing itself repeatedly, senselessly, against the rocks. How was I able to see it so clearly? I looked up and was surprised to find that the moon was shining. The rain had stopped. When? I hadn't noticed. I was soaked to the skin and shivering, my hair plastered to my head, water dripping into my eyes. I touched my face. Wet, lifeless flesh. Clouds tore across the heavens, but they didn't obscure the moon. I looked again at the sea. It wouldn't feel any colder than I was already. Seething, boiling, churning. Did I dare? 'Don't be so fucking stupid!' I said aloud, and walked away.

I passed Louise's house. If there had been a light in her bedroom I would have thrown stones at the window and made her come down; told her everything. Been mothered, soothed.

But the house was in darkness.

I went home, let myself in, and went straight up to the bathroom. They were still in the lounge, talking. I undressed, dried myself, and stared in the mirror. If I was, morally, such an ugly person as they thought, I'd surely look ugly. Paul had found me beautiful.

It's not designed and created for the sole purpose of producing descendants, I told myself. If it was, then after the acts of procreation it would drop off.

In bed, I hunched up into a foetus; I was petrified with cold. Later, when I'd thawed out, I started to feel randy. Extraordinary! After all the emotion of the past few hours I should have been completely exhausted. But the impulses obey no rules. I pretended I was Paul, and my pillow my own face.

Louise said 'If I were you I'd leave home.'

'I've been thinking about it.' Hardly surprising that I had: if for no other reason than being out of work. Surely there was more chance of a job in London, particularly in the winter when Bude was dead, from the neck up as well as down! A ghost of a place! Old ladies and their dogs, both animals and humans looking as if the end was nigh. I hated being on the dole! Hated it more and more! Not only because it meant no one wanted you, that you were consigned to a scrap-heap — a midden was the image that often occurred to me, a midden lousy and crawling with teenage rejects — but on the dole there was nothing to test myself against, nothing to stretch my mind or my body. It was as if some god had said 'These shall not grow up; these shall not be adults.' The crippling financial dependence on parents: another way of preventing growth. And that third barrier; the world of straight people, the law, that said 'Homosexual: thou shalt not touch another; thou shalt not learn to love.' At least not till the magic age of twenty-one. Though I didn't care a damn about what the law said. That wasn't going to stop me.

But how many rampant gays were likely to be flaunting themselves in the streets of Bude on a wet Wednesday afternoon in February? Dad's belief in corrupting influences was somewhat misplaced. Nevertheless, he and Mum made my life pretty miserable. On the few occasions I received a letter, her eyes almost drilled holes in the envelope. When someone telephoned for me, she always wanted to know who it was. I felt guilty doing the smallest thing, even a trip to Mrs Radford's shop for a bar of chocolate. I crept about at home, quiet as a mouse. The ten thirty curfew had to be strictly observed. And I didn't keep a diary any more. It wasn't worth it. I wondered how much longer I could stand it all. To leave seemed the only right course of action: I had nothing, absolutely nothing to lose by doing so. My parents had driven me to think of them as nothing worth losing. Appalling, that.

So I would leave. But not for a bit. I'd wait till the dust settled, till I could convince Mum and Dad that the reason I was going was to find work and not because I wanted to rush off, as a result of their discoveries, to some den of lascivious homosexual vice. It was the only way of keeping a link with them. I'd be welcome back. In spite of everything, I still wished them to love and admire me. And I still believed it was possible. Fortunately, they made no reference to what had been said. Not a single word. It was as if they had blotted it all out, erased it from their minds as the aborigines in New South Wales are thought to have done when they first saw Captain Cook and his ship: it can't be, therefore it isn't.

'I told my mum about you,' Louise said. 'And what happened.'

'You shouldn't have.'

'Why not?'

'Because . . . ' I was at a loss for an answer. I stirred the sugar round and round in the bowl, as if it might uncover the reason. We were in the Wimpy bar. The last day of February. Rain streamed down the windows; wind roared and funnelled along the streets. The epitome of depression. John fiddled about behind his counter, putting baked beans in a saucepan, just for something to do. Nobody was going to come in and eat them. 'I'm reconciled to being gay,' I said. 'It's stopped worrying me. I'm just as happy, inside myself, that I'm gay as you are not being gay. I want to love a man, live with another man . . . and I want sex with men.'

She was amused. 'I like the way you alter man to men when you mention sex.'

I laughed. 'Slip of the tongue. I don't know how to find what I want; I —'

'Are you sure? If you were really happy about it, you'd get on and do it.'

'Would I? There are other considerations.'

'Such as?'

'My parents. Now you've made me forget what I was going to say ! Why I wish you hadn't told your mother . . . I'm quite happy about being homosexual, but I don't want other people to know. I'm not ready, I guess.'

'They won't kill you for it. Mum was very sympathetic.'

'That's difficult to believe!'

'I wouldn't have mentioned it if I thought she wouldn't be. If you were her son, you'd find life rather different.'

'Well, I'm not her son, am I? Lucky old non-existent male child of Louise's mum and dad!'

'Don't be so bitter.'

'I'm angry. The whole bloody business makes me very, very angry.'

Louise's boy-friend arrived. Did he know? Hell, what did it matter if he did? What did it matter if everyone in town was sniggering behind my back? She was right. They wouldn't kill me. I was going to leave Bude anyway. I chatted for a few more minutes, then I thought I'd better depart. I didn't want the absurd complication of Martin feeling jealous! I said goodbye, and went out into the rain.

As I neared home, I saw a familiar figure inserting a key in the lock of the house next door. 'What are you doing here?' I cried.

'Ewan! It's great to see you!' He seemed thrilled I was there, laughing and smiling and gripping my shoulders. 'Come inside, for God's sake! I was afraid you'd be off working somewhere. I'm here for a couple of days . . . I haven't let on to Mum; I thought I'd make it a huge surprise . . . Cook the tea so it's ready when she's back from the shop.' He laughed again. 'Take off that wet coat. I'll put the kettle on.'

Alone with Leslie. What would my parents think? They wouldn't know , of course; they were out at work. That made it all so ridiculous: every day, from nine till half past five, I could be having orgies in my bedroom and they'd never guess.

He was still marvellously good-looking.

'What's happened in Bude since Christmas? Who's run off with whom? Surprise winner at Women's Institute bingo session? Anyone dead, married, born?'

'Nothing. Nothing.'

'That's what I thought.' He poured out the tea, and lit a cigarette. 'Still unemployed?'

'Yes. I'll have to follow in your footsteps and go to London.'

'Good money in the building trade.'

'I know. Your mum told my mum.'

'I'm a hod-carrier. Back-breaking work, but superb for the muscles. Look at my arms!' He flexed his biceps: hard as iron. 'How's your love life?'

'Negative.' I sipped my tea. I wasn't going to tell Leslie anything. Not yet. One day, perhaps, when I felt we were equal.

'Ewan, you must have done something interesting!'

'Have you?'

'I've enjoyed myself. I don't like London, but . . . well, I've made friends. Been out. Discos and pubs. Met a few girls. Though nothing I really want to see after breakfast-time next morning.'

I felt jealous, as usual. Inferior, as usual. Paul was right: Leslie *was* a bad influence. He destroyed my self-confidence. 'What about the girl at Newquay?' I asked. 'Anne. Do you ever see her?'

'No.' His face clouded. 'I miss her. Rather a lot. It was the best thing I ever did, clearing off last summer and going to Newquay. The job was rough, but at least I had some money. And it was a much better place for surf than here! Meeting Anne . . . sharing life, even if it was in a grotty bed-sit. It was a fabulous time!'

'I know. You've told me all about it before.'

'Have I? Yes, I suppose I have. Mum liked her.'

This was something I hadn't heard. 'I didn't know you'd

brought her home,' I said.

'I didn't. Mum came down for the day. They got on very well, the pair of them. She was a bit horrified — Mum was, I mean — by where we were living. Damp, she said; we'd get pneumonia!' He laughed. 'Load of nonsense!'

'You mean . . . your mother knew you were sleeping together? Didn't she mind?'

'I didn't *tell* her we were, but I suppose she guessed. No, she said nothing about it. Why?'

'Oh . . . no reason.' My parents, faced with such a situation, might possibly react in a similar way if nothing was pushed aggressively in front of them: of course, *we* didn't do that kind of thing, but the young don't have the same approach to organising their lives, what with the pill, and so on. It wouldn't strike them as abnormal; it wouldn't be such an affront to their morality that they would weep and faint, threaten to kick me out of the house for ever. That's the bloody problem with being gay; the difference of treatment, the discrimination! God! How it hurt just looking at Leslie and hearing him mention — almost as a triviality — those enviable things that were forbidden to me! It hurt! It *hurt!!*

Parents not minding you having a loving, stable relationship. Letting you bring your girl-friend back home, including her in the events and routines of the family. And if you got married, presents to help furnish a house. Hold hands anywhere. Kiss in the streets. Book a double room at a hotel and no eyebrows raised. But me? Others like me?

'I think I'd better be going,' I said.

'Why?' He was astonished. 'You've only just come! I haven't seen you since Christmas!'

'I have to do what you said you were about to do here. Start cooking.' I wasn't going to tell him the real reason: that just talking to him for five minutes upset me beyond endurance.

'See you tonight, then. Let's go out and get pissed. Well . . . at least have two or three pints.'

'I'm broke.'

'I'm not. I'll pay.'

'I . . . might have to go somewhere with Mum and Dad.'

'Ewan! What's the matter?'

'Nothing.'

I hurried out of the house. An old man, taking his dog for a walk, went slowly down the street. Leslie, indoors, preparing his mother's evening meal, knew only a little more about me than that old man. Could he imagine to himself what I'd been through? Everyone is alone. Particularly when they're in pain.

I changed my mind and went out with him that evening. Despite his ability to make me suffer, I thought I'd suffer more if I felt I was meekly obeying my parents' injunctions. Honour thy father and mother — or discard your oldest and closest friend. That made me want to be with him when, for other reasons, I might not have bothered. I decided on a full-frontal collision with Mum and Dad: I simply said where I was going and with whom. Which was greeted by complete silence from both of them.

Leslie had moved on. All that male teenage talk about sexual frustration, about girls who cavorted on the sand in brief bikinis being such a temptation, such a cause of agony that a law should be passed forbidding it, had been superseded by details of conquests, the length of the chase, and who was best at it. 'Doing my utmost to add to the copulation explosion,' he said with a coarse laugh. He'd grown up, in a way. Not in a very attractive way, though. Was it all true, I wondered, this boasting? Probably. But what of the girls as human beings, what about his own feelings? I knew Leslie well enough to realise that he was giving me a very distorted picture; being a sexual athlete wasn't his driving ambition. He was a one-girl person, basically. So why all this rather boring stuff? He hadn't adjusted from typical macho talk with his building-site mates, I guessed. Was there a female equivalent? I couldn't imagine Louise in the women's room swopping notes with Linda on the quality of orgasm. Girls were nicer than boys. More caring, more loving. Or were they? I had no more real idea of what went on inside the women's room than the old man I'd seen walking his dog had of what went on inside me.

On the third pint my tongue was loosened, and I felt both a

71

need to share confidences and a sensation of not being worried about the dangers of doing so. What was a best friend for, if you couldn't talk to him? Leslie wasn't easily shocked. The only thing that would unnerve him would be if I told him I fancied him. So I left that out. But I said all the rest.

His reaction was the same as Louise's: 'You must leave home!'

'I intend to.'

'You often *intend*, Ewan. But you hardly ever *do*.'

'Balls.'

'No.'

He was right. But he had no experience of the problems: in my shoes he would be the same. 'I don't know why I'm telling you all this,' I said. 'I'd decided not to.'

'I'd guessed. Some of it.'

'How?' He turned away, embarrassed. 'I was getting something out of it that you weren't?'

'Yes.'

On the fourth pint, when the room was beginning to spin, I said 'Do you wonder if you might be bisexual?'

'Because of what *we* did? The idea's never entered my head! To be quite honest, I wouldn't swear on the Bible that I'd never, in the whole of my life, do it again ... but ... it doesn't appeal, exactly! I like ... penetration.'

'I have experienced that too.

'With Louise?'

'Paul.'

He stared at me, a variety of different expressions flitting across his face. I had shocked him now. It's the hardest thing for straight people to accept: what gay men do in bed. His next remark was curious. 'Which way round? You ... screwed him?'

'No.'

'I don't want to hear any more!' He ruffled his hair, agitatedly. 'I can't ... stand the thought of that!'

On the way home the conversation was all about surfing. Had I lost him now; would we inevitably drift apart? I felt uncaring: the alcohol, probably. I was burning my boats, and it didn't matter. Being alone was no longer a misery. There was a kind of strength in it. Friendship with Leslie, with any heterosexual man, wasn't a delightful road stretching into pleasant, undiscovered country: it was a cul-de-sac.

I told my parents I wanted to go to London to find a job. 'Is this some mad scheme of Leslie's?' my mother asked.

'Nothing whatever to do with him! Why should it be? OK, he lives in London and he's working there. But I've been thinking about this for ages!'

'I would be surprised if you hadn't,' my father said.

I had not expected him to be an ally. I said, cautiously, 'What do you reckon, then?'

He didn't answer at once, but made a great business of folding up newspapers and emptying ash-trays. 'Have you thought what you might do when you get there?' he asked, eventually. 'Where you might live? Do you even know what the big city's like?'

'I've been there.'

'I'm not having you living with Leslie,' my mother said. 'Or with that whatever his name was ... Paul.' It was the first time since they'd found the diary that she made any direct reference to what she had read in it.

'I have no intention of living with Leslie,' I answered. 'Or Paul. I haven't seen or heard from him ... since ... ' I turned to my father. 'Dad, what do you say?'

He cleared his throat, took his pipe out of his mouth and put it back again. 'If none of that other business had happened, I'd probably say it was a good idea. Young though you are, and lonely and upset though your mother would be. But now ... I'm not sure.'

'Do you think it's fair to keep me on the dole for ever? Because that's what I'll be condemned to if I stay here!'

'Something will turn up,' my mother said.

'Pigs might fly!'

'I'll think about it,' Dad said.

I didn't really care if he thought about it or not: I had decided to go. If he wouldn't give his blessing, I would wait till my next social security giro arrived, then cash it and leave. Note-on-the-kitchen-table stuff. Hitch-hike to London. I could sleep on Leslie's floor to begin with, till I found my bearings. I didn't want to do that, not one little bit, but I didn't know anywhere else I could stay. Nor did I want to leave against my parents' wishes: the anguish it would cause, particularly to my mother. Christ! How adults manipulate their kids! Using the love and affection children feel to hang them in chains! But my love and affection, I was beginning to realise, had certain clear-cut limits.

A few days after this conversation, Dad said 'I've been in touch with an old friend of mine. I haven't seen him for two or three years, but I've known him for ages. Frank Sutton. He's a fireman. Three kids; girls ... the eldest, Tina, married six months back and left home. So they have a spare room. If you still want to go to London, you could live with them. You'd have to pay them some rent, of course. Nice people. You'd like them.'

'Whereabouts do they live?' I asked.

'Richmond. That's West London.' I knew the name, but I had no idea where it was exactly. 'What do you say?'

'I say yes!' I smiled and laughed. It was the first time I'd felt happy in his presence for weeks. 'Thanks, Dad!'

'Go and make peace with your mother. She's dead against the whole thing.' I was aware of that. I'd heard them arguing, through my bedroom wall at night, and though I couldn't follow what they were saying, the tone of her voice was usually querulous, his even and reasonable.

I *was* grateful. I could go because I was permitted to: which meant I could come back. As for Frank Sutton and his family, I didn't have to stay there for ever. If Dad had told them about the diary, and they tried to impose all sorts of restrictions on my movements, my stay wouldn't be long. But at least I wasn't doomed to be one of the teenage homeless, one of the thousands of unfortunate kids who drift to London hoping to find the streets paved with gold, and who discover instead dirt, poverty, drugs, despair.

I left one bright morning at the beginning of April. Not thumbing a lift with a few possessions in a rucksack; but on the coach, my fare paid by Dad, my clothes and personal things packed in two suitcases. Mum had been depressed and tearful since Dad's phone conversation with Frank Sutton. She'd convinced herself to a certain extent that my diary recorded a temporary lapse, that I regretted the folly of my ways, that I wasn't really like that at all. She now worried about drugs and drunkenness. Or was it a rationalisation of more profound feelings she didn't dare speak aloud? That the idea of being separated from her Ewan, her only child, her baby, was quite intolerable? She saw, I guessed, a life ahead of her that would lose some of its point and purpose, though the routine of things wouldn't be much different. She still had her work at the shop, her friends, keeping the house spick and span. But no Ewan: it was a savage wrench.

Though not for me. I was as excited as an eight-year-old at Christmas. On the day of departure, yes, some pangs, some butterflies in the stomach, even a moment of 'What the hell am I doing? I don't want to go at all!' Waving goodbye. Mum a small bleak woman standing on the vast expanse of coach-station tarmac.

Bude disappearing in the distance. Ahead, work and money. And other people like me. Bude out of sight. At *last* I could grow up!

Six: The Swimming-Pool Summer

Other people like me were thin on the ground. That's probably not a true statement: I mean I didn't go looking for them. Why not? Too much activity at first. Getting used to the bewilderment of London — its sheer size left me with a sort of permanent jet-lag — and trying to find work, trying to fit in with the Sutton household, and being a tourist gazing at Buckingham Palace, Westminster Abbey, the Houses of Parliament, the Tower, etcetera, etcetera. Paul had mentioned pubs and clubs and discos and their names had stayed in my head, as well as his comments about which were a good scene, which bad. Perhaps I didn't dare, yet. What would they expect of me, those other gays? Going out deliberately to search for them was quite different from the sheer chance of my meeting with Paul. I felt unable to initiate. And if someone else was the initiator and I didn't like him, how did I refuse? How could I avoid difficult, perhaps dangerous, situations? I was scared. Of people, I suppose; of relationships. Paul's legacy? Sex, quick and anonymous, would have been preferable. But I had no idea where that might be found. So I remained as chaste as my parents would have wished. Perhaps, subconsciously, I was still attempting to please them by not putting myself in a position where, if they knew, they could pronounce me guilty.

Life with the Suttons was, superficially, tolerable. Dad had told them: that was the fly in the ointment. They didn't mention it, but

I was convinced it was not my imagination; there was something a bit too obvious about the serious, silent way Frank Sutton looked at me, the fussy anxiety his wife showed if I didn't turn up at the exact moment I said I would be back. At night I was supposed to be in by twelve, but I never gave them any worries on that score. I hadn't found anything likely to keep me out after midnight; most evenings I was in their sitting-room, watching television. Though, when I could afford it, I went out for a drink, and, on two or three occasions, to the cinema with their daughters. Mandy was my age; Natalie a year younger. Dull, humourless, unattractive girls who spent most of their time doing their homework — they were both still at school — and who, when we did venture into the bustle of London, seemed as bewildered as I did. I decided that as soon as I could I'd get a bed-sit of my own. I resented the Sutton parents knowing, and I remained as aloof as possible, short of being impolite or surly. Mrs S. was the friendlier, but I didn't respond. There was little in her conversation, which was mostly about local gossip, the plants in her garden, and the behaviour of the Richmond Borough Council, to which I could respond.

Work was no easier to find than it had been at home. I hadn't expected to stroll immediately into a job which gave instant satisfaction and five thousand a year, so I told myself to be patient. Something will turn up, I kept thinking, echoing Mum. I explored more of London: Trafalgar Square, the National Gallery, Soho, Oxford Street, Kensington. I began to get acclimatised, to accept London's vastness: the fact that you couldn't see country on the horizon, and that beyond the horizon you would still be unable to see country. Richmond Park was a reasonable substitute; almost beautiful in late April and the beginning of May, with new leaves uncurling, deer grazing in the distance. I even got used to the noise. The first days and nights it had been impossible; Richmond was directly in the flight path of planes coming in to land at London Airport. To see Concorde, only a few feet — it seemed — above the Upper Richmond Road, was exciting, awesome: but night after night the planes disturbed my sleep. Eventually, however, I shut them out. As I did the constant roar of traffic.

And I discovered a gay pub in Richmond. Not one that Paul had mentioned; I found it by accident. I realised as soon as I'd ordered my beer: men looking me up and down, assessing my potential, I suppose. I didn't mind that. I did the same, every day, perhaps every hour of the day, walking in a crowded street. Just as straight boys do with girls they pass. At first, in the pub, I was nervous, then, after going in three nights running, disappointed. Nobody, not one person, spoke to me. In a sense that didn't matter: the man of my dreams — whoever he might be — wasn't in there. None of them measured up to Paul or Leslie for sheer good looks and sexiness. But the fragments of conversation I overheard gnawed at me inside: envy once again, gripping like a human hand. Parties, discos, boy-friends; who'd just fallen in love; who'd quarrelled irreconcilably: a whole complex mesh of relationships was hinted at, a way of existence that wove in and around the bigger, evident pattern of heterosexual living, but which remained unknown and unseen, except in here.

At the end of May I found a job. *A job!* Incredible!! Lifeguard at the local swimming pool. The superintendent was actually *impressed* by my qualifications. Nobody else employed there, he said, had life-saving certificates *and* first prize in a surfing championship. The pay was good, more than I expected. Soon I'd be able to find my own room! Freedom! Adulthood! And, I guess, a kind of job-satisfaction: Leslie and I had always been water babies; neither of us was very happy when we were away from the coast for long. I experienced pangs of regret whenever I thought of the beach at home: I could, at this moment, be surfing. Leslie probably was. He had said he would go back to Newquay when the summer came, work in a hotel and spend all his spare time in the sea as usual. Well . . . Richmond swimming bath wasn't the sea, but it was water: and the chance again to feel sun on my skin. My first job since the cafe, the summer I left school. It seemed light-years away!

It was not so glamorous as I had imagined. Life-saving duties were only a small part of the work, and on the days when the weather was dull and showery, there were few people to rescue;

in fact, during the whole time I was there, only one person got into difficulties, and as she was at the deep end of the pool and I was at the shallow end, somebody else on the staff dragged her out. And rather enjoyed, from what I could observe, giving her the kiss of life. Like all the other attendants, I was a sort of odd-job man. Weeding flower-beds, picking up litter, emptying bins, making tea and coffee, painting doors and a variety of other tasks filled my day. There was little of it spent strolling along the edge of the bath, watching the swimmers and pretending to be big and butch. Pretence it was: the other employees were huge hunks of bronzed beefcake who seemed to be perpetually adjusting their crotches. I was easily the thinnest, apart from Robin, the cashier. That was the only job we didn't do, taking in the money. The best activities were being a lifeguard when the sun was shining, and swimming in the pool when it was closed to the public. But picking up litter was nasty: after a hot, busy day, the discarded ice-cream cartons, bottles, plastic mugs and rotting bits of food were distinctly unattractive. Worst of all though was cleaning out the lavatories. The pipes from the cistern that flushed the water into the men's stalls had to be polished every morning with brasso. Not nice, when you thought of the hundreds of males who had urinated on them the previous day. Mopping the floor. And the lock-ups: often there was an absolutely disgusting mess that made me want to puke. And wonder that people should behave like that: they certainly wouldn't leave their own lavatories in such a revolting state. The morning of my eighteenth birthday started with that particular job. But on the whole I enjoyed being at the pool. My skin darkened with the sun, and I swam every evening, length after length — on one occasion thirty lengths — thinking of the right wave, on the beach at home, to go in the tube or ride till the sand ground me to a halt.

My fellow-workers accepted me, despite the fact that my body was puny compared with theirs. They admired my swimming ability, I think. In any case, they were more interested in persecuting the cashier than in taking the piss out of me. Robin, they said, was a poofter.

Whether he was gay or not I didn't know. He was about

twenty-four, slightly built, with short fair hair and blue eyes — very piercing blue eyes, with long lashes. He wasn't at all camp or effeminate, but anyone would look a bit effete beside the hairy apes we worked with. Robin was a loner: hardly ever leaving the booth where he took the customers' money and gave out admission tickets, and he spoke only when he had to. He didn't join us in our tea-breaks. On the few occasions when he left the turnstiles and went on some errand to another part of the pool, Dave, the most loud-mouthed of the lifeguards, would mince grotesquely in front of him, waving his arms and flicking his wrists, and make stupid comments like 'Lost your handbag, dearie?' or 'Watch it, everybody! Don't turn your backs to him!' Robin would walk on, pretending that Dave didn't exist.

These incidents left me with confused emotions: anger and disgust, but chiefly annoyance with myself for being too scared to protest. If Dave grinned and winked at me after he'd said 'She's lost her lipstick' or some other similar inanity, I'd grin back at him. I was frightened, I suppose: frightened that if I didn't respond, I'd receive the same treatment. On one occasion when I laughed at something Dave had said, I looked round and saw Robin staring at me, his cold blue eyes blazing with hatred. I blushed, and turned away. Why, I wondered as I went about my duties, did he look at me like that, whereas he regarded his tormentor with studied indifference? Because he thought I should know better than to collude with Dave? I did know better, of course: but what could I do? Perhaps it was something more subtle, though. If Robin *was* homosexual, he had perhaps guessed that I was, and that I was behaving like a traitor to myself. As a Jew might pretend he was a Gentile to escape torture during a pogrom.

One morning there was a lot of silly giggling and whispering between Dave and his mate, Trevor. 'I'll take it over to him,' Trevor said. 'He'll smell a rat if you do it.' He walked towards the turnstiles, carrying a cup of coffee. I followed; I had to get a key that had been left in Robin's office.

Robin looked up, surprised, when we came into his room. 'Here you are, darling,' Trevor said. 'A little refreshment. Make your short and curlies grow.' He laughed, and went out.

The saucer was on top of the cup. Robin removed it: warm urine. We looked at each other. Then I said 'I'll get rid of it.'

Robin's eyes blazed. 'You can sod off,' he said. I stared at him, hurt to the quick.

Two mornings later I had to clean out the lavatories. I heard the murmur of conversation coming from one of the cubicles: Dave and Trevor. I put my bucket and mop down, as quietly as I could. The cistern was filling, so it wasn't easy to catch what was being said, but when it was full the words were hideously clear.

'All you've got to do is to admit you're a poof,' Dave was saying. The tone of voice was eminently reasonable. 'Then we'll let you go.'

Silence.

'Lusting after little boys.' Trevor was speaking now. 'No wonder they have to keep you in the cashier's office. Just think what would happen to those poor kids if you supervised the changing-room!'

Silence.

'Hit him again,' said Dave.

Fist on flesh. A strangulated gasp. 'Fucking queer!' Thud. 'Fucking faggot!' Thud. 'Fucking fairy!' Thud.

'Pull the chain again. That'll cool him down.'

I banged on the door with the mop. 'I want to clean in there,' I shouted.

'It's only Ewan,' Trevor said. 'He won't say anything.' He laughed. 'If he wants to clean up, he can start on this creature.'

The door was unlocked. They emerged; Dave said to me 'That's what I'd like to see happen to all of them.' They went out.

Robin was upside down, his feet tied to the cistern. His hands were tied behind his back, and his head was dangling in the water of the lavatory pan. 'Christ!' I exclaimed. 'What shall I do?'

'There's a knife in my trouser pocket,' he croaked. I was about to cut the knots that bound him to the cistern when he said 'No, no! I'll crack my head on the porcelain! Hands first!'

When he was free and the right way up, I said 'Shall I call the police?'

He laughed. 'Don't be so bloody stupid!' He was shaking

uncontrollably; all of him, legs, arms, his torso. 'Fetch me a towel. It's opening time in five minutes; I can hardly let the public in looking like this.' His hair was saturated, and water dripped all over his clothes.

I found one in the men's changing-room. While he was drying his hair, I said 'What are you going to do? You can't allow them to get away with it! You can't!'

'Give up the job? Go back on the dole?'

'There must be something!'

'There isn't.'

'But why... why are they doing it? Why you?'

He sighed. 'I was in the pub one evening, having a quiet drink with some friends. Yes... you know the place; you've been in there. I didn't know who you were then, but I recognised you when you came here to work. Anyway, some yobs paid us a visit the night I'm talking about. Started being very offensive, making rude remarks about poofs and queers... They got turned out, but it was quite a scene: they smashed a dozen beer-mugs on their way to the door. The landlord should have phoned the police, but he didn't. So they came back later, with reinforcements. Including Dave and Trevor. The landlord did summon the police then, and they all went off, quiet as mice. Nothing happened. But for me the damage was done; Dave and Trevor had seen me and... that's it.' He shrugged his shoulders, a gesture of hopelessness. 'You can imagine what I thought of you grinning and laughing at what they were doing to me.'

'I didn't feel particularly good about it. I'm sorry. Very, very sorry.'

'Well... I suppose it's easy to say you should be honest and open, but when the chips are down it's bloody difficult. I might have acted as you did if I'd been in your shoes.'

'I'm sorry,' I said again.

He looked at his watch. 'If I don't open up I'll get the sack. There's always someone waiting to come in, dead on the hour.' He squeezed my hand, then touched my face. 'See you in the pub?' He smiled, a rueful half-smile: neither of us felt on top of the world at that moment.

When I arrived the next morning, Robin was not in his office. Nor was there any sign of Dave and Trevor. I hurried into the lavatories; the same cubicle door was shut: Trevor and Dave uttering the same obscenities. This time I must *do* something, I said to myself. But what? I ran out, hoping to find the superintendent. That could be difficult: he wasn't always on the premises, which was probably why the two lifeguards had found it easy to bully Robin and remain undetected by anyone in authority. The superintendent didn't often turn up when we did, at nine a.m.; sometimes he wasn't there till noon, and if business was quiet, he would leave after an hour. I was in luck, however: he had just parked his car and was coming through the turnstiles. 'There's been an accident in the men's toilets!' I shouted.

'What's happened?'

'It's the cashier!' I rushed off, not wanting to answer any questions.

I waited by the entrance to the lavatories. 'What is it? What's going on?' he asked when he caught up with me.

'In there,' I said, pointing at the locked cubicle.

As soon as they heard our voices, Trevor and Dave came out. There was not much else they could do; staying inside would have seemed even more suspicious. Robin was kneeling on the floor, looking like a drowned rat. They hadn't tied him up this morning, just shoved him to his knees and pushed his head into the lavatory pan.

'You two — into the men's changing-room,' the superintendent barked. 'And you'd better have a pretty good explanation!' They shuffled away. 'Robin! get up and dry your hair. Then go to your office. I'll have a word with you later.' He turned to me. 'You! Get a bucket and mop and swab this place out. It doesn't look as if it's been touched for a month!'

'I cleaned it yesterday!'

'Well, you can do it again today!'

I did as I was told, but very quickly; I wanted to find out what was going to happen to Dave and Trevor. Dismissed on the spot, one of the other attendants said; perhaps they went over the mark with Robin, just a little bit, but people like that cashier deserved everything they had coming to them; didn't they?

The superintendent was walking over to Robin's office. I followed, anxious to know what they would have to say to each other.

The office was not a particularly private place. It was a one-roomed building, with windows on three sides. One faced the pool, one looked out into the car park, and the third was by the turnstiles. The weather was hot, so all three windows were open. It was ten to ten, I noticed; a queue of people was already forming by the entrance. As I approached, I could hear Robin and the superintendent shouting. What on earth was happening now? I stood against a corner of the building and listened.

'Damn it, man!' the superintendent was saying. 'They must have had some reason! What sort of provocation did you give them?'

'I didn't give them any!'

'They told me ... well, to put it bluntly ... that you're queer. That you like small boys.'

'I'm not the least bit interested in small boys! It's an *outrageous* accusation!'

'Maybe, maybe. People can invent absurd excuses to defend themselves; I know that. But the point is ... I can't afford to take that kind of risk. This is a swimming pool, Robin. Paid for by the rate-payers; their money keeps it going. Suppose Dave was telling the truth? There could be a nasty scandal and I'd be held responsible. Now, I want to know. Are you a homosexual?'

Silence. Tell him you're not, I begged inwardly. Tell him you're not! It doesn't matter, lying about yourself. Why chuck away a good job?

'Yes,' Robin said.

There was another silence. 'Collect your cards on Friday. I'll have your wages made up to the end of the month. Which is generous.'

'You can't do that!' Robin shouted. 'I haven't done anything wrong!'

'I can't afford the risk! I've told you already!'

'What risk? There isn't any risk! Do you think I can seduce half

84

a dozen people in here while I'm selling tickets? That I'd even *want* to?'

'Don't be ridiculous.'

'I shall appeal. I'll write to my MP! I'll go to an Industrial Relations Tribunal!'

'That won't get you far.'

I couldn't stand it any longer. What I did next was without thought, the result of indignation I couldn't restrain. I kicked the office door open and yelled 'You can sack me while you're at it! I'm one of those horrible, nauseating people you call queer! And I'm *proud* of it!'

Robin smiled.

The superintendent looked utterly bewildered. 'I think the whole world's gone mad this morning,' he said. 'What do you mean by bursting in here like that? What the hell are you doing?' Normally he was a mild, not unpleasant man; indolent and easy-going. He expected his swimming pool virtually to run itself, without his having to check up and harrass his staff. But now he was flushed and breathing heavily; his hair had flopped forward over one eye, and a vein in his temple throbbed. 'Get out of here at once, Macrae! Go back to your duties, or I'll sack you for insolence and insubordination!'

'You don't need to,' I answered. 'I've already resigned. Jesus! Do you really think any decent person would want to work here now?'

I walked out, through the turnstiles and into the street. The queue of people had grown; some of them were becoming restive: it was gone ten o'clock and the doors were not yet open.

Robin came after me. 'I certainly underestimated you,' he said. 'My God . . . you change quickly!'

I looked at him, puzzled. 'I don't know what you mean.'

'Last week you were joining in the laughter at my expense. Today you've talked yourself, I mean *bawled* yourself, out of a job when you could easily have kept quiet!'

'I don't know why I did it,' I said, and leaned against a parked car. I felt sick. 'Something just boiled up in me. Maybe I'll live to regret it.'

'I doubt that.'

'Well...we've been honest, I suppose.'

'A good starting-point for leading a reasonable life. Listen...what are you going to do now?'

'Back on the dole, I imagine. And you?'

'I didn't mean that. We've got the whole day ahead; that's what I was thinking of. What shall we do with it? Look...come round to my place and have something to eat. I've had no breakfast this morning.'

He lived in an untidy attic on the top floor of a large, rambling Victorian house; it was the sort of room a painter might use as a studio, particularly as the view was magnificent: a picturesque clutter of roofs and chimneys of all shapes, angles and sizes, and — beyond — the Thames threading its way through what seemed like a vast expanse of trees which defended it from the incursions of the factories and houses stretching on, one would think, for ever. I was staring at almost the whole of West London. 'There are some marvellous sunsets,' Robin said. 'Spoiled by aeroplanes, of course. Some nights the floor shakes with the noise.' The room itself was badly in need of redecoration, and the furniture was old and shabby. The curtains looked as if they would fall to bits if you touched them. There was a double bed, a wardrobe, a table and chairs. An antique gas fire. On the mantelpiece, various ornaments and some framed photographs. Pictures on the wall: a still life and Van Gogh's *Sunflowers*. Clothes, books, records, dirty plates scattered everywhere. The kitchen was tiny, off the landing, no bigger than a cupboard. Robin had offered me breakfast, but he didn't appear to be in a hurry to start cooking. He was sitting on the edge of the bed, hands over his face, shivering.

'What's wrong?' I asked.

'Shock. I think. It's just beginning to catch up with me. I was so struck by what you did it sort of postponed it.' He held out his hand, and I put mine against it. 'Come to bed with me.'

I was so surprised I didn't know what to say. 'I'm not sure if I fancy you,' I answered, after a moment's silence.

He looked at me. The blue eyes were now sad and defeated.

'I'm ugly?'

'No.'

'Haven't you ever been to bed with someone for reasons other than sexual attraction? Out of affection? Or because the other person at that moment so desperately needs you to touch him and hold him he'd maybe lose any sense of reality if you didn't?'

'No. I'm . . . how can I describe it? . . . very new to it all.'

I held him: he shuddered as if he were ill or freezing, and though he made no sound, his tears were wet on the skin of my throat and my shoulders. Gradually he calmed, and rested against me, just breathing, as if all the hurt he had experienced in the past few days was beginning to ebb. Now I did want to make love to him, not because I felt randy, but to tell him it was all right now, that not everyone in the world was vile, sick and brutal: I wanted to help heal the wounds. So I screwed him, because that was what he seemed to be asking me to do. The first time in my life I'd done that. Peace. I lay there, quite still, feeling sane and alive and clean. It was good to be Ewan, I said to myself, and good to be here doing this. I'm no longer a muddled kid: this is man's estate.

'Do you want to get dressed?'

'No.'

'Neither do I. But I must find some fags.'

I watched him walking about the room, and I wondered why it had never occurred to me before that he was beautiful. Slim, well-proportioned, graceful in his movements. A human's toes, the curve of an arm, the knobs down a spine, the way a shoulder-blade shifts under the skin, can make you stare because they each have something in them of perfection.

He came back to bed, and we smoked and talked. Talked for hours. The history of our lives. He was brought up in Woodford, on the other side of London, the third of four brothers all straight except for him. All married now. His parents didn't know and he wouldn't dream of telling them. School he hated, shining as the dunce of the class. Then a series of dead-end jobs. He liked disco dancing, classical music, reading. A solitary, but not from choice. 'I remember when I was about fifteen,' he said, 'I was in the changing-room at school. We'd been playing rugby, which I loathed. I suddenly realised, Christ! I'm looking at these boys in the way I'm supposed to look at girls.' And there was nothing, he said, absolutely nothing he could do about it, no one he could speak to; it all had to be smothered up inside. 'I reckoned I was unique! A genetic mistake, like a mongol. Oh God . . . the misery of those years!'

'What happened?' I asked. 'Eventually?'

'It's a bit easier in London, I guess, than Bude.'

The knowledge, gained slowly from snippets of conversation accidentally overhead, that there were gay pubs and clubs and discos, that there was a newspaper called *Gay News*; but what made him 'come out'(an odd expression,I thought)was seeing a notice, a small round sticker in fact, on the window of a telephone kiosk, advertising an organisation called Icebreakers. Depressed, lonely and unhappy gay men and women, it suggested, should ring them; it printed the number. He did, after dialling it four times and putting the receiver down because he was so scared of what he might be doing. He laughed. 'Was it an invitation to an orgy was my main fear. To be blackmailed. But it was almost unbelievably prim and proper. A very sweet, gentle, middle-aged man giving a Sunday afternoon tea-party in his elegant Regency house in Camden Town, trying to calm the nerves of a dozen extremely worried people, who were as terrified as I was at the thought of how vulnerable they might be making themselves.' He laughed again. 'I've travelled a long way since!'

'How old were you?'

'Seventeen.'

He had hundreds of gay friends and acquaintances now. But he'd been on his own this past nine months, since James had moved out. The real love of his life, I guessed from the number of times and the way, bitter but also affectionate, in which he referred to James. This attic had been their home. Its untidy, almost dilapidated condition, he said, was because the heart had gone out of it. Since James had left he'd existed rather than lived.

'He was black.'

'Black!'

'Yes, the colour of soot. All over. I used to call him Kwango. You sound surprised.'

'I've never thought before about blacks being gay. Or Chinese, or Russians, for that matter.'

'There's no reason why there shouldn't be gay Tibetans or Eskimos.' He was amused. 'I *know* a gay Tibetan, in fact.'

'There's a great deal for me to learn, I'm beginning to realise.'

'I envy you.'

'Why?'

'The voyage of discovery is very pleasant.'

'Yours hasn't finished.'

'True. But I didn't bargain for being mangled by thugs and losing a job. James would simply call it one of the risks. Of being homosexual, of leading a gay life. But I don't see why the hell it should be.' He got out of bed. 'I'm going to find something to eat. Are you hungry?'

'Starving!'

'Man cannot live by words and sex alone.' He looked at his watch. 'I promised you breakfast, but it won't even be lunch! A cross between lunch and tea. Stay there; we'll eat in bed.'

A fry-up: bacon, eggs, tomatoes, sausages, and toast. And a bottle of red wine. It was much more pleasant than cleaning the toilets at the swimming pool, but tomorrow? The dole queue. And before that, the Suttons. I didn't want to move: the bed was warm, and it had Robin. More attractive than any other kind of existence I could visualise for myself.

Hours passed. Robin talked about oppression and gay militancy. His friends. Old lovers. Good clubs. Clubs that were nothing but a rip-off. We had sex again. 'Are you staying the night?' he asked.

'I can't.'

'Oh yes, you can! Go back now and tell those nice but not very sympathetic people you're lodging with that you've found somewhere else to live. Collect all your stuff and bring it here. Then we'll go out, find a not too expensive restaurant, and celebrate. After that, we'll return to this room and . . . you'll be able to stay the night. Easy!'

I stared at him. 'Don't joke with me!'

'I'm not! I mean it! I need someone to help pay the rent.' He laughed, and said 'I don't need any old person to help pay the rent. But this place is lonely ... and I think I want *you*.'

'You'll regret it.'

'That's in the future.'

Inside me, stars danced: mad, I said to myself, mad; what do you know about him, what are you letting yourself in for? But, if you don't leap at what's possible, what's offered, you'll end up with nothing. Nobody had offered me anything before. I kissed him. 'I'll try not to make you regret it. Ever!'

'That doesn't matter *now*. And don't ever talk about ever! You'll regret *that*.'

He smiled and ran his forefinger across my face. 'Your eyes!'

'What about them?'

'Alight.'

On the bus, half-way home, I thought: what on earth was I going to say to Frank Sutton? And ... would I be able to cope with the memories of James?

Seven: Coming Out

These questions, I found out, didn't matter. The first led to a very uncomfortable half hour, but once I had packed all my things and gone I pushed it out of my mind. James was a problem that took a bit longer. Robin made his own position totally clear from the start; I would never be able, I was glad to realise, to use accusations of deception against him. Neither emotional deception — a common human crime is to say 'I love you above all other; I will love you for ever' when something else is meant — nor that of any other sort: financial, sexual, a misplaced desire to flatter and please. James he loved above all other, and he said so. If there was a possibility of the black man returning to him he would unhesitatingly say yes. They still met and talked, usually in a crowd at the pub or at a party; it was as if they could not really leave one another alone. As far as I was concerned, Robin thought of me as a friend he enjoyed living with and sleeping with. If ever we wanted someone else, he said, we should, both of us, be honest enough to say so: hiding feelings and pretending no attraction existed when it obviously did, was a sure recipe for the destruction of the relationship.

'You'll be hurt by what I've said,' he added.

I was. It seemed to me a very peculiar way of behaving. But over the next few weeks, as I examined what I felt and thought of the implications, I discovered that it was my ego that was bruised, not my emotions. I wasn't in love with him — he wasn't Paul — any more than he was with me; it was circumstances that had driven us together, not an all-consuming passion. He wasn't my 'type', sexually — Paul and Leslie were. It didn't work out in bed; we both wanted the same thing. We were, neither of us, initiators; and screwing just simply didn't satisfy me, bring any real pleasure or happiness, except on rare occasions. It bothered me still that I wanted a so-called 'passive' role: I wasn't a woman, in no way thought I was born in the wrong sex, in no way wanted to act like a woman. The signals I gave out were totally male, and my behaviour and all my preoccupations I considered just as masculine as Paul's or Leslie's. 'Just get on and enjoy it while you have the chance,' Robin said, when I told him of my worries. 'You've been brought up to believe that because you've got a cock it automatically has to be shoved into something. Conditioning, that's all. If you don't want to do it, then don't. There's no law about it. And if you want a great big cock up you, then go out and find one. There's no shortage, as far as I can see.'

It was good advice. I was still the same Ewan Macrae; *more* of the same Ewan Macrae when I was being fucked, being what I now knew I had always wanted to be: fulfilled, adult, complete. So I slept from time to time with the attractive men who smiled at me in the pub, hoping always that one of them would be that special person I'd fall in love with, another Paul. None of them was. That didn't upset me very much: time was on my side; I could wait. And living with Robin was relaxed, easy, and open: fun. One day in the future I would be dispossessed from the flat by James; of that I was sure, and the thought made me sadder than the fact that my love life was mostly a series of one-night stands. When James returned I hoped I'd have the strength to be alone. It would be wrong to want to cling, barnacle-like, to the first rock I had gripped.

I was astonished that Robin, from time to time, still made love with James. I had thought that the black man would be the one person he wouldn't sleep with, unless they came together again on a permanent basis. But astonishment was a frequent reaction as I began to explore the gay scene with Robin. His friends became my friends. He had no heterosexual acquaintances. 'I can't be bothered any longer,' he said. 'The pretences! The masks you're forced to wear! And if they know, they think they're the ultimate in tolerance, which is patronising.' He had no one like Leslie. The curiously tangled relationships his friends had were to me extraordinary: not at all what I wanted for myself. Monogamy was rare, though it did exist. Strange polygamous states were more prevalent, triangles, even quadrangles; or total promiscuity, or affairs that lasted a month, a week, before another was tested and that found wanting. Everybody at some time or another, I felt, had slept or would sleep with everybody else. Was this just cosmopolitan London? Did it in any way resemble the heterosexual world? It wasn't easy to imagine people behaving like this in Bude.

But they seemed as happy as anyone else. My entire upbringing — which, of course, recognised marriage between one man and one woman as the only possible avenue to bliss — suggested that such a way of life as I was now involved with was like Dead Sea fruit; sterile, unfulfilling, the primrose path to everlasting misery and a VD clinic. Mortal wounds that were not only self-inflicted but inflicted by others on others. Yet quarrels, depressions, jealousies were not all that common. These people were remarkably unbitchy. The petty backbiting, the no-holds-barred vindictiveness, that are tags hung by the straight world on the gay, did not, as far as I could see, exist, except at a joking level, when one man would score off another like a cat sharpening its claws on a chair, just to keep his wits keen.

I discovered, too, that limp wrists and handbags, mincing walks and wiggling bottoms, were mostly a myth invented by straights. Not that they were totally absent: but they were used more as an act, an entertainment gays put on for each other in the places they met, rather than a mode of existence outside. The desire to outrage the straight world by imitating the stereotype of heterosexual assumption in, for example, Putney High Street on a busy Saturday afternoon was, if not as rare as a black one-legged nun driving a Morgan, rare enough. There were uniforms and stereotypes, but only other gays would see their real implications: the men in leather were not Hell's Angels, the ones in camouflage not deserters from the white Rhodesian army, the moustachioed clones with short back and sides and nondescript plaid shirt and jeans weren't having a quick drink before returning to their wives in Twickenham and Teddington. Uniforms exist everywhere: the fawn coats, brown suits, beige pullovers and tan shoes of young middle-class farmers in Bude trying to look smart on a night out; or the long flowered frocks, the dyed permed hair and imitation jewellery of middle-aged women going to the theatre or their husband's firm's annual dinner.

Maybe at this time I was just naive, but would the comments one might make about the sad and sordid, or the joyous and fulfilling, aspects of gay life be very different from any strictures or panegyrics on human behaviour in general? I doubt it.

We both found jobs quite rapidly. Not through the labour exchange, but through friends of friends of friends. One interesting function of the gay community, I learned, was its ability to help its own members, almost as Jews or West Indians or Freemasons do. Somebody had usually heard of somebody who could put you in touch with a gay plumber, a car mechanic, an electrician, or a television repair man who would do what you asked more quickly, and possibly more cheaply, than people you contacted through the yellow pages.

Robin got work as a clerk in the tax office. 'Deadly dull,' he said, 'but at half past five I can switch off and forget it completely. And the money's just slightly more than it was at the swimming pool.'

My job was a bit more esoteric: assistant stage manager (in theory), general dogsbody (in practice) for a dance company. It operated on a shoe-string budget, touring in the outer suburbs of London; its studio was a ramshackle church hall not far from where we lived. The hours and the pay were, to put it mildly, unpredictable. So were the members of the company. The director and sole choreographer was a fierce old woman, a real dragon with close-cropped black hair and a man's voice; she tended to regard as a personal insult anything that the company was interested in that was unconnected with dance, and activities that might lead to someone being late for rehearsal or want an hour off she treated as sabotage. Her husband, who wore an ill-fitting red wig, was, though he was much too old for it, the company's male lead. He could do no wrong, as far as the director was concerned; his mistakes (which were more frequent than those of any other dancer) were always somebody else's fault. The rest of the company, in a different way, were just as weird. They took themselves so seriously. They lived for their art — breathed, ate, and slept it. Which was undoubtedly meritorious, but they were in the habit of thinking their productions, and the whole philosophy that lay behind what they were doing, were vastly superior to anything put on by the Kirov or the Royal Ballet. Margot Fonteyn was, to them, a fourletter world. The company could not afford an orchestra, and as it was illegal to use taped music without paying royalties, they danced to a cacophonous assortment of noises they recorded for themselves: bangs, crashes and whistles that sounded like blocked drainpipes in agony, or pigs being subjected to medieval tortures. These curious pieces were given names like 'Summer Night' or 'Fragment', or one-syllable abstractions: 'Art', 'Space', 'Planes'. Similarly with the decor: they could never pay for a set, so it became a virtue not to have one. All this economic difficulty was elevated to a spurious kind of excellence: dispensing with real music and scenery made it possible to move nearer the realm of 'pure dance', whatever that was.

Pure hocus pocus was my opinion. Not that I ever said so. I got on with my job — operating lights or the tape recorder, brewing tea, checking seating arrangements, hiring minibuses, darning holes in costumes, preparing salads (they were all ardent vegetarians and obsessed by the need to diet), finding cigarettes at crucial moments — anything that no one else could do at the time. But it seemed to me to be a severe case of the emperor's clothes. Particularly in the pauses between the grunts and gasps that emerged from the tape recorder: the grunts and gasps of the dancers then became embarrassingly audible, like overhearing other people's orgasms. That was intentional, I discovered; it was all to do with 'the total experience'. I was surprised that anybody wanted to come and see such rubbish, but it wasn't unusual for an audience to consist of two or three hundred earnest-looking souls who imagined they were plunging into an important, if obscure, cultural extravaganza. I found it difficult not to laugh as I wondered who was the most deluded — the audience or the company. Whatever turns you on, I suppose: the human species, I was beginning to realise, was capable of an infinity of variations as far as that was concerned. Though why? It would have been easier to understand if someone in this outfit was laughing all the way to the bank, but nobody was.

My relationship with my parents at this time was very strained, indeed almost non-existent. My mother, in the past, had called me 'the jewel in her crown'; I had hurt her once by saying that my father should occupy that place in her affections. But I felt I had been like some precious gem, treasured, kept carefully in a drawer, an insurance against middle age when my mother — grandmother as she looked forward to being — could view with satisfaction her son, married, with children, mortgage, and a safe, steady job. She would never be able to reconcile herself to the fact that I was not a machine for fashioning other Macraes. Many gay people regret that they won't have children: not me. My mother's assumptions, and my efforts to copy her behaviour, her moral and sexual attitudes, had imprisoned me in that drawer. But I had escaped now.

I wrote, giving my new address, and said, briefly, that I was sharing a room with a friend because I was happier there than at the Suttons. I waxed eloquent about the charms and comforts of the new lodgings, describing in detail the splendid panorama I could see from the window. But she was not taken in. Nor was my father. Letters arrived, reproachful, threatening: it would kill them to think I had returned to my bad old ways; they were depressed, and when was I coming home? I asked Robin's advice. But he had little sympathy, and could scarcely conceal his impatience. 'Tell them you're being screwed by every dishy man in London,' he said. 'They're using emotional blackmail. Which is as contemptible as real blackmail.' It was more complex than that, I felt; they loved me, and cared about what happened to me. As I loved and cared about them. One day I hoped they would understand. And accept me, not just grudgingly, but so that the numerous pleasures and joys of a relationship between parents and sons could again be experienced. 'You're asking for the moon,' Robin said. He was a great one for cutting losses. I was driven to write that they were making it very difficult for me to return, even for a weekend; this produced a frantic reply, and I stopped writing for a while. Eventually I wrote a non-committal three pages, chiefly about the weather. (It was late August, and hot; London sweated and struggled for breath in the grimy heat.) There was no answer. In October I sent my father a birthday card, but that also elicited no response. I was now more angry than sad.

But I felt so inwardly well balanced that distress and indignation were emotions I could cope with; they didn't disturb the happiness of that time. Living with Robin had given me belief in myself. Apart from the pleasures of friendship and sharing a home, I found, with guys I met in the pubs and the discos, a relatively contented sex life. Sexual misery, it began to dawn on me, was one of the most destructive of human conditions; it pervaded every area of activity, sapped the ability to concentrate, the will to do anything other than seek an end to frustration. For the first time in years I could work, read, enjoy people's company, listen to music, dance for hours at a club, and devote *all* my energies to what I was doing.

At Christmas we decided to repaint the attic, and make new curtains, lampshades and cushions. We didn't start the job, however, for another six months. When it was finished, we sat there for ages, admiring our efforts. 'I like that mushroom colour,' Robin said. 'It soothes.'

'At home we never eat mushrooms. I was sixteen when I first ate one. With bacon and chips in a Wimpy bar.'

'Why?'

'My mother is so frightened a toadstool might have slipped in by mistake that she never buys them. That way, she feels there's no chance of being poisoned.'

'Like never crossing a main road because a car might knock you down. She's round the bend, your mother.'

'No. Not really.' It annoyed me, hearing him criticise her. Though what other reaction could I expect after what I'd said? His comment was not unreasonable. I was the irrational one here: it was quite all right for me to tear her character to bits, but no one else was allowed to. Robin wouldn't do so, of course, if I stopped making unfavourable remarks, but that was difficult. One has to talk to someone. I hadn't in any way come to terms with what I felt about my parents. I should have gone home for a weekend: but that was easier said than done.

'James wants to know if he can leave his car outside. He has to do some major repairs and it isn't possible where he's living now. Do you mind?'

'I don't own the house. Or the road, for that matter.'

'But do you mind?'

'Not at all. Are you . . . the two of you . . . any closer now?'

'If we were, I wouldn't have agreed to all this refurbishing of our room. *Our* room, Ewan.'

He was telling the truth, but the moment James parked his decrepit, rusty Triumph Herald by our front door, I felt my days in the attic were now numbered. His leaving it there seemed to me a kind of claim being staked, an unspoken message that said if he couldn't yet resume permanent quarters inside the house, he was only a foot or two from the door-bell, waiting. At weekends and on several evenings — it was now high summer again; Robin and I had been living together for a whole year, and I had just celebrated my nineteenth birthday — James's long legs protruded from under his car while the rest of him, invisible, banged away at whatever it was that he had to do to his exhaust box or his track-rod ball joints or the bottom of his oil sump. Invisible, but not inaudible: he was always either singing or swearing. Then coming indoors to wash, and sometimes he would stay and eat with us, or accompany us to the pub.

I could understand what Robin saw in him. Very sexy, and all of a piece, without any problems of any sort. He was more relaxed inside his own skin that any white person I had met. Mentally and physically serene, but given to marvellous extrovert outbursts of energy, whether dancing, arguing, or just laughing and joking: it was an exhilaration that left me envious, made almost everybody else I knew look anaemic. I could easily imagine him in the place where I thought his origins were, some tropical island paradise, so I was very surprised when he said he came from Stroud in

Gloucestershire. A native West Country boy like me. He was twenty-five, a postgraduate student at London University, doing a Ph.D. in physics. Another error: I had assumed a West Indian immigrant job, on the buses or a porter at a railway station.

I liked dancing with him. Indeed I liked dancing, period: now I could be on the floor with other boys rather than with girls, I stopped worrying about clumsiness, or what did she want from me. Inhibitions that had sometimes spoiled straight discos at the age of sixteen vanished and I found my legs and my arms, my whole person, more and more part of the music. It was an unwinding process in which the self ultimately became an expressive instrument, moving, moving, moving, in patterns and sequences that perpetually changed and developed, grew simpler or more complex; body and music, dancer and dance, an inseparable entity. The gay clubs: their ridiculous names, suggestive of all sorts of heaven on earth, their cheap glitter and high prices, their lights subtle enough to deceive everyone into thinking everyone else was good-looking ('Never stay till the finish,' Robin said. 'Unless you want to see how unattractive the boy you've landed up with really is'), the crowds of lonely men waiting for Mr Right to walk through the door, eyeing every newcomer and only seeing Mr Compromise, the pick-ups, the rejections, the certainty for most of only a one-night stand at best: oh yes, it was easy enough for me to feel superior, going as I always did with Robin and James and a crowd of our friends (their friends, in fact; without Robin, would they include me?) and never being at a loss for someone to dance with. James in particular.

When I found that I very much wanted to go to bed with James, I thought long and hard about my relationship with Robin. It was obviously time to go, and leave the two of them together. Lovers: we hardly knew any lovers, not in the proper sense of that word. And it wasn't surprising: they didn't haunt the pubs and the clubs as we did. They stayed at home, entertained their friends, sat in front of the television, and whatever the multitude of activities and hobbies they might pursue, they only occasionally needed to be part of the gay scene, or indeed any kind of scene. They were, simply, themselves and each other. The feelings James produced in me were dangerous: I was beginning to fall in love, a dizzy, delirious sensation that made me gasp for breath. And wasn't I using Robin as a crutch, my entrée to the gay world? I ought to stand on my own two feet. I watched James and Robin at a distance as I danced with somebody else and saw glimpses of long, serious conversations, noticed them touch each other, a caress on the arm or a kiss.

And as Robin said nothing, I decided it was up to me to broach the subject.

'You're right in what you've thought,' he said. 'We could be together again tomorrow.'

'Well ... why aren't you?'

He frowned. 'We haven't exactly worked out what the relationship should be. Though I know what I want.'

'One to one, no casual sex with other people, and to hell with pubs and clubs and discos?'

'Yes. That's certainly part of it. I don't know about James. He *says* that's what he wants, but I'm not sure.'

'Why not try?'

'Mmm.'

'Look ... don't take this the wrong way. I haven't met anybody else, nothing like that. But I think I need to move on. Be alone for a bit ... stop doing everything as if I was your shadow. Can you understand? I'm sort of ... flexing my muscles or something.'

'It was inevitable, right from the day you moved in here. But ... where are you going to live?'

'I'll find a place.'

'If what we're talking about really does happen, I should be the one who goes. Not you. I've already discussed it with James. He agrees.'

I stared at him. 'You really are incredible!'

'Why?'

'You're so ... what's the word I want? ... good.'

'Oh, for Christ's sake!'

'I don't think I shall ever meet anyone I'll respect so much.'

'Balls! And shut up, will you! You're making me feeling acutely embarrassed!'

A week later he went. I couldn't decide if it had come about because of our own inner needs, or whether we'd manipulated each other into a situation from which it was impossible to withdraw. James arrived to help with the packing; he was in an odd mood, uncommunicative and a little morose. At one point, when Robin was in the kitchen, he looked up from what he was doing — fixing the travelling screws in the record player — and gazed at me, a solemn, mournful expression in his eyes. He seemed to be trying to say something, but what it was I couldn't fathom. Surely he didn't regret what was happening now? Robin for his part, could scarcely conceal his excitement. James knows I fancy him, I said to myself. It must indeed be obvious. I blushed, and turned away.

When they had gone the room looked pitiful. Almost empty, except for the basic furniture — the bed, the table, the chairs and the wardrobe belonged to the landlord — and I suddenly realised how little of this place had been mine. It was as if some beautiful thing, that had become what it was by a slow process of organic growth, had been mutilated. Robin-and-Ewan was dead, James-and-Ewan impossible. I didn't like the idea of living here now. Absurd! I was just as responsible for the present situation as Robin or James. Hell! It's what we all wanted! Or thought we did.

I was absolutely free to do as I wished. I was on my own, and the dance company was not working for the next month; it was having its summer break. What to do with this freedom, this ability to choose anything, accountable to nobody, unencumbered by any obligations? I had a little cash in the bank. I could go abroad if I felt like it. Another new experience! I had never left England. Or I could throw myself into a frenzy of pubbing and clubbing, play the scene for all it was worth.

What I did was on the spur of the moment; indeed if I'd stopped to think I wouldn't have done it. I went home to Bude, arriving without any prior announcement on my parents' doorstep.

To say they were delighted to see me would be a gross understatement. It was the return of the Prodigal Son. They cross-examined me about my job, what shows I had seen in London, whether I was looking after myself and eating properly; was my living accommodation adequate: all the usual questions any parent might ask of a son who has been away a long time. I was told the local gossip — a year's births, deaths, marriages, separations and divorces. My father proudly showed me his garden (a good summer for soft fruit, apparently) and my mother explained why she had re-arranged all the furniture. Conversational small talk flowed with ease. The important subjects were avoided.

Mum, however, was anxious to find out why I had selected this particular moment to reappear; she obviously thought that something of a serious nature had happened: and one evening when Dad was out of the way she asked if I was in any sort of trouble.

'No,' I answered with a smile. 'What trouble should I be in?'

'I don't know, Ewan. But is there? Anything . . . you feel you should tell us . . . the law, for instance.'

'The law?' For a moment I was baffled, then I understood: no sex before twenty-one. A more idiotic, cruel law, in my opinion, would be hard to imagine. A boy and a girl were legal at sixteen; why not people like me? 'I told you already,' I said. 'I've a month's holiday. I've come down for a few days; that's all.'

'What's happened to . . . to your friend, the one you share with?'

'Robin? He's moved. I live on my own now.'

'Well . . . maybe that's for the best.'

'Why?'

'Not a very good influence, I imagine.'

'You don't know anything about it, Mum. And for heaven's sake, I'm beyond the age of being influenced! Would you like . . . to discuss it? Robin?'

'No. No! I don't want to hear! Ever!' The deep feeling in her voice saddened me. Appalled me. Only a Ewan who could utter decent platitudes about the weather or the neighbours was acceptable; what was beneath could not be mentioned in case she discovered it really did exist. Ours would always be a pathetic apology of a relationship. Mother and son! More like a couple of acquaintances who might talk to each other because they happened, once, to have lodged under the same roof.

'You're still making it difficult for me to want to come back,' I said.

I had inadvertently touched a very raw nerve. She flared up: 'I think that is an extremely unkind thing to say, Ewan! After all we've done for you, to tell us you don't want to be here! The ingratitude of it! It leaves me ... speechless!'

'But you *don't* want me. You want Ewan, yes, but someone quite other than what I am, some imaginary child of your own invention, not the real me!'

'I'll say this: whatever trouble you're in, we'll stand by you. We love you.'

Silence. I should have left it there; I should have been tactful, discreet — and dishonest. 'You don't love me,' I said. 'I can't believe you do. Because if you did ... you'd take me as I am. Love should be stronger than all your loathing that I'm gay.' She burst into tears. 'I'm sorry; I went too far. I shouldn't have said that.' I wished I could touch her, hold her hands: I thought of the easy warmth between so many people I knew, but in my family we never touched. It wasn't considered proper behaviour.

'I don't think you're a bad person.' She sniffed and dried her eyes. 'Only ... very muddled. Very bewildered.'

'I'm not.'

'Tell me ... can you honestly say that you're happy? I don't mean in the sense of ordinary everyday things going right or wrong. I mean *really* happy.'

'Yes. Now.'

'I just can't believe that.'

I sighed. The conversation was over. But it was the first of several, all more or less the same. The gulf was impossible to bridge.

Leslie was at home. I was glad to escape and seek out his company. He had injured his back, surfing; the only cure for it was to rest. He disliked losing even one day on the beach, and this enforced holiday meant that he was not only missing the best part of the season, but several championships as well; nor could he continue with the job he had had the previous summer — teaching people to surf. He was fed up, angry with himself, and therefore delighted when I appeared. He had come a long way since we'd shared first prize two years ago; he was now the junior champion of England. I had hardly touched a board in that time, whereas he, apart from hod-carrying in the winter, had spent almost all his daylight hours in the sea.

He'd filled out; a man now. Bronzed skin, hair almost white from the sun, salt in the lines on his face: the healthy, all-male beach-boy. He'd taken to smoking a curly pipe, which made him look not quite himself. It was a pose, a macho signal. I surfed, a clumsy amateur now, while he, the cool professional, stood on the sand, commenting on my mistakes. In the evenings we went out drinking. He was going on holiday next week, to Greece, island-hopping. By himself; he didn't really know anyone he wanted to go with. Except me. 'Greece is cheap,' he said. 'Much cheaper than here. I'd like you to come! We ... seem to have picked up the threads. I don't know anybody else I'd rather be with. Ms Right, I suppose, but *she* doesn't seem to be anywhere on the horizon.'

"I'll think about it. I'm not sure I can afford it.' That wasn't quite true: I'd done a rapid mental calculation, and discovered I had just about enough money. The idea, in fact, appealed to me very much. But ... and it was a big but ... how would we get on with each other? I was determined that never again would I be put in a position where I'd feel second-rate, jealous, angry with both myself and him.

'You've changed, Ewan.'

'How so?'

'Much more sure of who you are.'

I told him some of the things that had happened in the past twelve months, and I listened to the story of his nineteenth year. There had been no time, he said, for a proper love life; it had all been hard work, earning money and surfing. A few sexual adventures, but nothing that had lasted more than a week. He was tired of that kind of thing: ready for something totally different.

Next day I said I would go with him. He wasn't able, any longer, to make me feel inferior: I was enjoying his company as much as I had when we were kids. We were equals now. I felt elated, a surge of joy, when I realised that not one flicker of jealousy remained. What happened in Greece has already been written about in *The*

Lighthouse, so there's no need to repeat it here. Leslie found what he'd wanted all his life, or what he thought he'd wanted — a girl called Victoria — then panicked when he came back to England, feeling he couldn't cope with having achieved his heart's desire, and he nearly lost her for ever. Indeed he did lose her; it was only the accident of his mother's sudden death that brought them together again. I met Christos, a man so hairy you could hardly see any skin. He took me to Rhodes, which I'd never have visited otherwise. A holiday companion. Nothing more.

In the autumn, when Leslie returned to London, we decided to share the attic. It wasn't a good idea, and he moved out after only a week; he couldn't stand my life-style, he said. It might be truer to say that our very different life-styles would never make it easy for us to occupy the same room: a house, yes. Which we now do, very amicably. But a gay and a straight in one room! It was stupid even to think it would be possible. I was behaving a bit madly at the time, I suppose. I plunged briefly into a hectic life of pub, club, and promiscuity. I dyed my hair yellow, and wore all sorts of outrageous gear borrowed from the dance company's wardrobe. I got used to waking up in other people's flats in various parts of London. Or, when I found nobody to go back home with, I'd limp into the attic in the small hours of the morning, and crash out in one of the armchairs. Was I now trying to prove something to myself? No. It was a bit like the reason why people tackle Everest: because it's there. I was lucky not to get the clap, or worse.

But maybe it's something everybody has to do at least once in their lives. There is an excitement: every first time has promise, anticipation; maybe this man tonight will fulfill *all* your dreams. And, though he never performs that function, you can say you were not rejected, not one of the ugly and unwanted, left unchosen at two a.m., going back alone to your unlovely bed-sitting-room. Why do the unchosen almost always remain unchosen? Not necessarily because they are hideous to look at, but in some indefinable way the mysterious processes of sexual selection mark them out as flawed. Is it inhibiting shyness that makes it impossible for them to approach or to be approached? Or age: forty plus in the gay world can be as grotesque a disfigurement as lacking an eye.

I soon grew tired of it. I said to myself, I've done it; I know what it's like: it's time to stop. The repetitive rituals became so tedious. Bath, choosing clothes and after-shave, drinks in tatty dimly-lit dancing-places at absurdly inflated prices; who would I pick, who would pick me, your place or mine? A naked body, particularly in the intimacy of the bedroom, is always interesting; none is quite like any other. But the procedure, when it's possible to have sex with almost anyone, was for me becoming sterile and meaningless, not even physically very exciting.

I don't care if I never see the inside of a gay club again, I said to myself as I danced one Saturday evening, wanting to leave the floor but not doing so because it was Gloria Gaynor, and, old though it is, everyone invariably dances to that one. Why? The words, I suppose; they speak so directly to gays: *I will survive.* Leaving my partner rather abruptly when it finished, I cannoned head-on into a very tall black man. James! 'Dance with me,' he said. *Lullaby of Broadway.* Well, I couldn't resist that one either. Or James, for that matter. My stomach knotted up; I felt dizzy.

'Where's Robin?' I yelled over the music.

He shook his head. 'Not here.'

'How is he?'

'Later. We can't talk against this.' Goodnight, baby; goodnight, the milkman's on his way. 'Your song,' he said, smiling.

'How do you know that?'

'Robin told me.'

'Oh.'

When it stopped, he said 'Can I come back with you tonight?'

I was amazed. 'Why?' was the only answer I could think of.

He laughed. 'I left some things in the flat.'

'Oh yes?'

'Under the bed. Have you ever looked under the bed?'

'No,' I admitted.

Eight: James

'I can't believe it!' I cried. 'So much waste of feeling! Of time! Of . . .' I looked round at the things of my room. To a stranger, to James even, it would seem occupied by someone in transit, living out of a suitcase. 'Of all this.' I was remembering it as it was, comfortable with Robin's possessions. 'Of Robin himself.'

'There's no blame to be attached. To any of us; him, me, you. You can't bend feelings, make them fit expected slots. You know that, better than any of us.'

He and Robin had split up. For ever: finally, irrevocably. Right from the beginning, the reconciliation had not worked. Robin had given up his job and emigrated. To Australia: as if he needed to put the greatest possible distance, half the world, between himself and James. It was sad that he had not tried to get in touch with me, but, to put it mildly, I could understand his reasons. I was the unwitting cause of it all.

'Do you know why I worked on my car outside this house?'

'I believed what you said. That you couldn't, for some reason, do it elsewhere. And that you wanted to be near Robin.'

'That's the truth. Then I started to fancy you. In a vague sort of way. Perhaps I was curious: wondering what Robin had found. You misinterpreted all the signals.'

'When did I become more than a potential bit on the side?'

'I don't know.' He yawned, and rubbed his hands over his eyes. It was late: three a.m. I was exhausted. Physically and emotionally. The misery and suffering that had been revealed, the possible excitement and happiness of the future — I looked at both blankly, almost objectively: I was too tired to react, to take it all in. 'As soon as Robin left here,' James said. 'Then, certainly. Your face, your body . . . voice, gestures . . . everything haunted me. All the time. Everywhere. At the university. Having a bath, cooking a meal. Most of all . . . in bed.' He stroked my arm. 'These last few weeks have been agony. Inflicting pain on somebody else. Twice.' For a moment he looked haggard. Then touched my face and kissed me. The effect was electric: rousing something at my absolute interior that had never before been stirred. 'Maybe the day I helped him move out of this room. It was . . . shutting a door. On a sunlit garden.'

'I remember.'

'Remember what?'

'How you looked at me. The sourness of your mood.' I was silent for a while, yawning myself. 'You don't think,' I asked, 'that Robin . . . will do anything stupid?'

'Try to kill himself?'

'Yes.'

'He isn't the type. You don't book a passage from London to Sydney in order to do that.'

'But if he finds nothing when he gets there?'

'Sydney, I'm told, is a good place for gays.'

'I've never fancied it.'

'Ewan . . . ' He glanced at his watch. 'It's late. Do I have to go home now?'

'No. But I only want to sleep.'

'So do I.'

'Have you looked under the bed yet?'

'What?'

'As I thought. A way in.'

He peered underneath it, pulled something out, and held it up for me to see. A small roll of white carpet, a remnant, of no use at all. 'That has been there since . . . oh, long before you met Robin. You've never noticed it?'

I laughed. 'No.'

'Now I've discovered what limits there are to your house-cleaning abilities.' He put it down on a chair. I started to undress. 'It may come in handy some time. You never know.'

'What, a thing that size?'

'Why not?' He unzipped his jeans and stepped out of them. I trembled. 'You and I, one day, could have a bedroom carpeted wall to wall in white. Do you like that idea?'

I nodded.

There is no such thing as perfection and it is often our own fault that there is not. The next few weeks might have been that, but I could not escape a sensation of illicit and stolen pleasures, of guilt. I worried about Robin a great deal. I tried to convince myself that I wasn't responsible for what had happened; that in no way was it my doing. Simply the fact that I existed and had come into their lives at a certain time had been the cause. Or was it? If not me, would it have been another person? Possibly. I wanted to feel responsible, in Robin's debt: to do something that would ease his pain, this person I respected so much. I suppose in order to ease my own. James and Robin had tried to repair a thing that was smashed, but there were too many pieces missing. I wished I had his address. But what could I have written? Or he in reply to me?

'Stop bleeding,' James said. He was teaching me to drive at the time; I had just stalled his car at some green traffic lights.

'I will. But it has to take its natural course, I think.'

It did. But it's buried somewhere inside me, and if I dig it up and look at it, I do so still with a sense of shame. We never heard, either of us, from Robin; not even a postcard.

Some people leave an indelible mark on you, an imprint of themselves like Christ's face on the handkerchief. An Irish boy I spent one night with and never saw again, a boy who'd picked me up at a disco, pale-skinned and red-haired with vivid green eyes, spoke to me of Ireland, of soft rain and wet green grass, of big clumsy potatoes just lifted from the soil, the red dust still on them. It was not in his words. His only remark about Ireland was that he'd never been so glad in his life as the day he'd stood on the

Holyhead boat, watching Dun Laoghaire recede. Our conversation was mostly banal. Though I was interested that he was a practising Catholic who attended Mass every Sunday, went to Confession and took Holy Communion: and never once admitted to the priest on the other side of the grille that he had sex, promiscuously, with men. 'That's my own private affair,' he said. 'Between me and God.' I thought no more about it as we made love. It was rain, grass, and clumsy potatoes his body spoke of; I could almost smell the earth, the red dust. I felt sad afterwards. I wanted to see him again; he'd given me something of himself, something important. He, evidently, did not think so. In the morning he was impatient for me to be gone.

Leslie was the same; I had experienced the essence of him: merman, water baby, beach-boy, surfer. The smell of the sea. On every inch of his skin it was written. Victoria knew that.

But not Robin. Robin had left no such impression, nothing of himself. It's very difficult, therefore, to describe him. I can't even see him in my mind's eye. Not once had I glimpsed that essence, and maybe that's why I could never love him as I did James. And perhaps why he, of all people, attracted the attention of the queer-bashers. They saw something they could they thought easily destroy.

Skin and silence and touch communicate more than words. James's mark, his imprint, changed me. Branded me. Before I met him, if I'd been at the point of death, I'd have said nothing in my past life would make me want to live it a second time, but now I would say it had all been worthwhile, if only for the best half dozen times with him in bed. Though there is far more to it than sex. There are no words I can find to explain adequately what he means to me.

Such a filthy people, some say of the blacks, those who cannot find anything in anyone who does not reflect their own self-satisfied image. His absolute difference from me is perpetual fascination. I shall never unlock the whole secret of it. I like studying the palms of his hands, paler than the rest of him, as if the patterns of lines were ancient runes that might one day yield up their meaning. It amuses him. 'What do you see?' he asks.

'Rum and banana boats? Feathered bodies in a tribal dance?' Something of that, I guess, though I never say so. 'It's like bat's skin,' I tell him. How ignorant are those people who talk of the sterility of homosexual life; of the impossibility of real satisfaction, mental, emotional, spiritual, physical! A story of when he was fourteen, a comment about badly cooked carrots, his breath in my ear, discussing music or stained-glass windows or the people next door, watching him laugh across a room full of people, the sound of a syllable left hanging in the air: they are all bits of the mosaic that is him. Straight people are scared that it isn't sterile, that something other than a baby can be a wholly satisfying end-product of love.

If our relationship is like some sort of narrative that has a beginning, a middle, and not yet an end, discovering each other's past is as if the book stops for a moment, and one observes a photograph, a lantern slide, that has nothing to do with us as a pair, but which has helped in some small way to our being together. So he learned of my meningitis summer, of Leslie, Louise, my parents. And I of a primary school in Stroud not unlike my own, of grey Cotswold cottages that more than any other houses grow out of landscape. Of student life in London. His family. Mother, father, two sisters (one married, one still at school). They all know he is gay. Have accepted it without difficulty, have even made his boy-friends welcome at home. He had told them when he was seventeen. Though he'd been aware, long before, of what he was. From the age of twelve he was certain, and prior to that he'd had some idea. 'We were eating cold beef and pickles at the time,' he said. 'A Monday. For twenty-four hours my father was a bit stunned. But my mother said so long as I was happy, then she was. Though she feared I would not be. The world, she pointed out, was not disposed to like or even tolerate homosexuals.'

'I find it incredible!'

'I was in love. Quite hopelessly, with a boy called William. I needed to talk, and my parents listened.'

'I've never heard of such a thing! Is it to do with being black?'

He roared with laughter. 'Of course not! I've met a few others, all whites as it happens, who are equally lucky with their families. Not very many. Mostly the opposite. And one friend whose father refuses to believe that homosexuality even exists!"It's all in the mind," he says. "A myth. A deep American plot."'

'A deep *American* plot?'

'Yes. A variant of reds under the bed. An invention of the CIA to sap a nation's morale.'

'Never, in a million years, will my parents be happy about me! Never!'

'I've been with mine to gay clubs. Dad gets bored, but Mum is fascinated. Not that she understands. She looked round the club in Cheltenham and said "This room is full of gorgeous men!" I agreed; yes, it was. "Don't they realise almost any girl would go weak at the knees?" Perhaps they do, I told her, but so what? They aren't interested. "I shall never work it out," she murmured. She has this theory, you see, that you take up with your own sex after some disappointment with girls. There's nothing I can do to shift that idea from her mind.'

'The thought of my parents raving it up in a gay club is mind-boggling! Ludicrous!'

'We often joke about it. Once, when I was telling my father some involved story, he said, "James, your life sounds like an everyday story of sodomy." Not *every* day, I answered. Robin was with us, one Christmas, swopping recipes with my mother. A cosy domestic conversation. "I stuffed a marrow last week," he said. A slip of the tongue, he told me afterwards; he had meant to say he had *cooked* a stuffed marrow. "Really, Robin?" she said, laughing. "Whatever did James do that night?"'

'What a difference it must make! There'd be no guilt, no low self-esteem. Just ... be happy!'

'This Christmas, we'll visit them in Stroud. Would you like that?'

'Yes. Yes, I'd love it!'

'And ... next Easter, or in the summer, we'll stay with your parents. It's time we sorted them out.'

'We'll ... *stay* with them? No. Oh no! It would be quite impossible! A recipe for disaster!'

'We'll see about that.'

He isn't easy to live with. We don't fit domestically, as Robin and I did. We have rows. He's unpunctual. Domineering. Sometimes he goes off on his own. I don't know where and I don't ask, because it doesn't really matter. His thesis has to be written this year, and he sits up half the night, working. Which makes me feel lonely. We lived in the attic at first, but I was never entirely at ease with him there: too many memories of Robin. He warned me that it would be difficult to move out. Rented accommodation in London, he said, whether it was furnished or unfurnished, was almost impossible to find and the prices sky-high. And even if we did discover somewhere suitable, we might not get it: some people objected to two men sharing. 'Landlords think that if they let a room to gays,' he said, 'every queen in London will be trolling in and out with her poodles. And I'm black as well! It isn't worth trying.' But I did try: and found he was right on every single count. A gay negro: a double cripple in society's eyes. Let him have a room in their house? Send him back to Trinidad — if they'll take him! Though that was not what people actually said, I could feel it under their words.

Often he can be infuriating. One evening the lights fused. 'You're the physicist,' I said, expecting him to repair the damage at once. 'Let James be, and there was light.'

'Dark. Ebony all over.'

'I know.'

'I'm a theoretical physicist, not a practical one.' He lit a candle and went on reading. I had to stagger about in a dusty cupboard under the stairs and learn to do it myself. I was angry. Of course he must know how to mend a fuse! Twenty minutes later I had solved the problem; light was restored. 'So you've had a physics lesson,' he said, calmly blowing out his candle. 'You can't expect to go through life totally ignorant of these things.'

'Are you?'

'Of course not!'

I threw a cushion at him.

On Christmas Eve, when we were at Stroud, Mrs Radford died. A heart attack. Leslie was there, at home, when it happened. All he could think of was to find Victoria. He hitched a lift across Devon on Christmas night, and arrived in a state of collapse at her parents' house — numb, cold, and so upset he was scarcely aware of what he was doing. He poured out a jumbled, hysterical tale, the thread of which was 'For Christ's sake, help me!' And they did.

He turned up, unexpectedly, at the attic, one evening at the end of January. He was selling his mother's house, he said. And with the money he was buying a place in London. In Kilburn. There was a vast difference in the prices, but he was hoping to take out a mortgage to cover that. Would I, he wanted to know — he had never met James before, and was eyeing this long, loose-limbed black man rather warily — move in as a lodger to help pay the mortgage?

Some months later, we — James and I — did so. We have the whole upstairs; it's a self-contained flat, with a grandstand view of other mean little dwellings. But our home. Easy to cope with: it's so empty there's almost nothing to sweep and clean, apart from the floors. James borrowed a hundred pounds from his parents; that, and the little money we had, bought us, second-hand at sales, some basic essentials: bed, an electric cooker, table, chairs, a paraffin stove. A few odds and ends since, when we've been able to afford them. But we're a long way off carpeting our bedroom wall to wall in white.

I've rented a colour TV. I was able to do that because I changed my job, and I'm earning a little more than when I worked for the dance company. A new job was essential: the church hall in Richmond was miles away from where we are living now; the cost of travelling would have been astronomical. And I'd hardly have seen James. When it was Robin, that didn't matter, but it was different now. I found work — as a milkman!

On my first day I kept thinking how I'd love to compare notes with Dad. Not that he would be proud; he always looked to something better for me than following in his footsteps. But I enjoy what I'm doing. It's easy; it's out of doors, and there's no one supervising me all the time. Unlike Dad, I have to get up at five a.m. But I'm finished by early afternoon, which means that unless James has gone in to the university or disappeared on one of his solitary walkabouts, he and I have a large part of the day together. I'm often so tired in the evenings that I fall asleep in front of the television. When that happens, he undresses me, picks me up as if I were a baby, and carries me to bed. Which always seems to turn him on, for the next thing I know is he's screwing me like mad. 'I'm too exhausted to resist,' I mutter. 'Rape!'

'Shut your eyes and think of Trinidad.'

I open them, look at him, and kiss him.

James is a bully, and he takes an enormous pleasure in organising my existence. He nagged, on and off for weeks, about visiting my parents. 'Don't mention me,' he said. 'Just let them know you're coming. And when we arrive, say you've brought a friend with you. They won't *eat* us, for God's sake!' Eventually I agreed. What had I to lose? Nothing, or next to nothing; my parents and I had drifted apart, almost totally. 'I'm not going to switch on a lot of synthetic charm,' he said. 'But I can show them I'm not a primitive savage who's just dropped out of a tree.'

'You *are* a primitive savage,' I answered. 'And, besides, they've never even heard of you. Let alone your being the colour of soot.'

'Well, it's about time they did.'

'I'm warning you . . . on your own head be it!'

I took a day's holiday, a Friday. James was more or less his own master now his thesis was finished. Leslie and Victoria were in Newquay: I wrote to tell them what was happening, and they replied that they'd come up to stay with Little Michael, who had recently married his Juicy Lucy, and give us moral support.

It was not exactly an easy weekend. My parents have no particular prejudices about colour, though that is accidental rather than considered: I don't expect they've ever thought about it. The subject has not been part of their lives; it isn't an everyday occurrence to see a black person in Bude. They guessed immediately what the relationship was between James and me, and the colour of his skin may well, in the circumstances, have added an extra dimension of horror. I don't know: it wasn't discussed. Nor was the dreadful problem of homosexuality even hinted at. We spent the time, the four of us, simply being polite to one another: careful and non-committal. James and I tried our best to give no offence; didn't touch or kiss, and certainly didn't sleep together. I was in my old bedroom, he downstairs on the sofa. It was all a great strain, and it was good to escape and spend a few hours with Leslie and Victoria, to relax and be our normal selves.

My father and I did swop milk roundsmen's stories. Which was pleasant, though he said he was disappointed I hadn't found a more worthwhile job. He seemed to have forgotten that when he was my age there was no unemployment, that nowadays people are grateful for almost any kind of work. And one entertaining diversion occurred: the lights fused. James immediately leaped into action. 'Now a man with a first class honours degree in physics should be capable of doing something about that,' he said to me, and asked my father to show him where the fuse box was. Not only were the lights on in next to no time, but he was able to point out what had caused the fault. He went round the house looking at plugs and sockets. 'The entire system is very old,' he said. 'And dangerous. It needs re-wiring.' He suggested that if Dad bought the necessary cable he would come down one weekend and do the job for nothing. An offer which Dad accepted.

'You're a bastard,' I said, when we were on our own.

He grinned. 'Yes. Isn't it fun?'

They could see, I suppose, that we were sane and happy, not the monsters of popular myth, though I doubt if they'll ever accept us for what we are. But I'm glad we're trying. They are my *parents*, for God's sake! How can you discard parents — whatever they think of you — and feel one-hundred-per-cent happy about it?

Leslie had given up attempting to teach James the rudimentary skills of surfing. I was amused that something I thought was as easy as breathing my lover found impossible. I lay on the sand, beside Victoria. Leslie and James started to wrestle with each other.

'They're so physical, those two!' she said. 'It wears me out, just being near them.'

'It's a good thing they get on so well. It could have been awkward, sharing the house.'

She sighed. 'I don't suppose it would have mattered. We're hardly ever there.'

'Everything OK with you and Leslie?'

'Of course. Couldn't be better.' She looked at me. 'You often ask me that question. As if you were expecting it not to be.'

'Will you marry him one of these days?'

'Yes.'

'Christ!' I was extremely surprised.

She laughed. 'When I've got my degree. I've one more year at Cambridge. Though I can't see us having babies, not for a long time. I want to work: I'd like to go into publishing. You'll be the best man, of course.'

'Isn't that . . . rather up to Leslie?'

'We've discussed it; it's what he wants. He's very fond of you. He's spent all his life measuring himself against you. He still does. I don't think he's as adult as you are. You've outstripped him in so many ways.'

'It was quite the opposite, four or five years back. Apart from his parents dying, he's never had to suffer.'

'I wouldn't say that.'

'You should have known us at sixteen!'

'I've heard.'

'Have you?'

She nodded. 'Everything.'

'Everything?'

She was silent for a moment, then said 'Do you still fancy him?'

'Yes. Not that it bothers me. I am . . . rather occupied elsewhere! Does it bother you?'

'Not in the slightest. I asked him once, when we'd had a row, if he'd prefer to go upstairs and sleep with you two intead of me.'

'I wouldn't have kicked him out! Nor would James.'

'Men . . . do you ever stop being tom-cats?'

'What did Leslie say?'

'Well . . . I wasn't exactly being serious! He thought I was, and got very worried that I imagined he would like to.'

'And *would* he?'

'No. Not in a million years. So he said.' She laughed. 'Tough luck, Ewan!'

'I always wondered if he was bisexual.'

'It's possible. Even probable. You and James...you both certainly seem to have something. Will it last?'

'Oh, yes. For a long time. All the foreseeable future. Do you doubt it?'

'No.'

That evening I overheard a conversation between Mum and Dad. 'One day he'll settle down and marry a nice girl,' she said. 'You see if I'm not right!' Dad's answer was inaudible. And maybe unprintable.

The foreseeable future. I had long since grown out of thinking that it was worthwhile making plans. Nothing can last for ever. James and I might get bored, break up, fall in love with other people. Nobody is your own private property; people are only lent to you. But the longer you're together the harder it must be to part; you stay because of shared possessions, shared routines, or you can't face the emptiness of being yourself, alone. All the wrong reasons. Learning to be happy alone: that's probably the most difficult thing of all about growing up. Not the problem of 'I'll survive' but of finding the strength to be sufficiently fulfilled without the prop of a lover, a wife, or a husband.

There's a wonderfully huge amount of life left to me: fifty years, if I'm lucky. All the adult decades. I'm twenty; I haven't even started!

But the milkman's on his way.

other novels by David Rees published by GMP:

THE HUNGER

Ireland in the late 1840s, where a beleaguered population falls victim to massive famine following the spread of an uncontrollable potato blight. Against this harsh background of turmoil, starvation and disease, an English landowner and an Irish peasant struggle to keep not only themselves and those around them alive, but also the love they feel for one another in a society and era which violently condemn it.

ISBN 0 85449 008 6   £4.95

THE ESTUARY

Luke, an extremely attractive but selfish young man, surprises himself when he gets involved with an older man after breaking up with his girlfriend.

'Highly readable and once begun is difficult to put down. It examines sympathetically and realistically the complexities of homo, hetero and bisexual relationships and the irrationalities, uncertainties, doubts and suspicions which surround love and sex. Highly recommended' – *Time Out.*

ISBN 0 907040 20 9   £3.95

other recent fiction from GMP:

Jeremy Beadle
DEATH SCENE

The discovery of Guy Latimer's mutilated body in an alleyway near one of London's leading gay nightclubs opens this intriguing and compulsive novel. It soon becomes apparent that the killing was premeditated and that the assailant must have been known to the victim. Suspicion falls on Guy's circle of gay friends, all of whom seem to be hiding crucial information, but who soon find themselves obliged to join forces to try and solve the killing, fearful of a set-up by the police.

A highly innovative and cleverly plotted mystery that in classic whodunnit style grips the reader until the very last pages, with a dramatic final twist. The first of a new genre – a contemporary gay murder story set in present-day Britain, with sharp observations on both the nature of the gay community in post-AIDS London and on the reactions and attitudes of the wider community around it.

'Beadle's writing is adept and assured, the characters are well-drawn and plausible ... I recommend it as a rattling good yarn' – *New Musical Express.*

ISBN 0 85449 088 4   £4.95

Timothy Ireland
THE NOVICE

New fiction from this award-winning author.

Donovan Crowther is 23 years old and still a virgin. Romantic and uncertain, he is drawn to London in his search for love. And from the moment he arrives in the capital, it's clear that whatever happens, his life will never be the same again.

Donovan's experiences will be all too familiar to the many who have taken the same path, yet Ireland achieves a level of intimacy with the reader that is disarmingly immediate.

'Ireland ... has a way of capturing the immediacy of emotional experience, with all the attendant confusions and contradictions, without ever resorting to hackneyed sentimentality or galling set formulas. A talent to be reckoned with' – *Time Out*.

ISBN 0 85449 089 2   £3.95

Also from Timothy Ireland
WHO LIES INSIDE

... It was as if out of the corner of my eye I could see a stranger standing in the shadows and I was scared to look too closely in case I saw who it was. Worst of all the stranger seemed to have wriggled under my skin, or had grown inside me all my eighteen years; only now for some reason that stranger was not content to stay in the shadows but wanted to step out into the light and be seen ...

The much acclaimed novel about growing up gay, winner of The Other Award for fiction in 1984.

'This is an exciting, innovative book which deserves the widest possible readership – it will open your eyes to some issues about gay men and must be made available to young people themselves' – *ILEA Contact*

ISBN 0 907040 30 6   £3.95

A T Fitzroy
DESPISED AND REJECTED

This major piece of gay literary history was first published at the height of the First World War. Focusing on the brutal persecution of conscientious objectors, and with its two main characters a lesbian and a gay man, it was almost immediately banned. This is its first reissue in Britain for seventy years.

In a new introduction written for this edition Jonathan Cutbill examines the background to the novel and the trial of its original publisher.

'A sophisticated and well-crafted novel' – Sunday Times.

'A thoughtful and well-considered book...brave and pioneering. Compelling fiction about a world that may seem light years away – but from which many attitudes still prevail' – *Gay Times*.

'Fitzroy presents the socialist-pacifist cause with intelligence and passion and manages to avoid sentimentality. She entertainingly lampoons the social pretensions, patriotic double-think, snobbery, smugness and bloodlust' – Peter Parker, *Times Literary Supplement*.

ISBN 0 85449 063 9   £5.95

James Purdy
IN A SHALLOW GRAVE

When they sent Garnet Montrose to Vietnam they told him he'd go out a boy and come back a man. But he comes back a freak, so hideously scarred that no one can stand to look at his face. The explosion which destroyed his company has skinned him alive.

Living as a recluse on a storm-battered Virginia farm, he dreams of the days when he was eighteen and king of the local dance hall, kept alive by his obsession with the untouchable Georgina Rance, his childhood sweetheart still living down the road. It seems this half-life will never end – until the arrival of the mysterious Daventry, offering him total love or total destruction...

'...a lyrical mystery, unsolved because unsolvable, but crammed with a sense of spiritual beauty at work in the physical world. James Purdy is more than just a good writer. He has created his own genre of rhapsodic horror stories' – *The Pink Paper*.

'Mr Purdy writes like an angel, with accuracy, wit and freshness , but a fallen angel, versed in the sinful ways of men' – *The Times*.
'A marvellous tour de force. A novel that engages as it entertains, draws the reader in as it draws something out of him' – *Publishers Weekly*.

ISBN 0 85449 093 0   £4.95

Rohase Piercy
MY DEAREST HOLMES

Although Dr Watson is known for recording nearly sixty of his adventures with the celebrated Sherlock Holmes, he also wrote other reminiscences of their long friendship which were never intended for publication during their lifetimes. Rescued from oblivion by Rohase Piercy, here are two previously unknown stories about the great detective and his companion, throwing a fresh light upon their famous partnership and helping to explain much which has puzzled their devotees.

'Thoroughly amusing...Wonderful stuff' – Stanley Reynolds, *The Guardian*

'Any Holmes aficianado would enjoy it for its own sake' – *Gay Times*

'These pieces work on a number of levels – the detective story (written in a style amazingly close to the originals), and the social document. Most importantly, a literate and humane portrait of one man's love for another' – *Gay Life*.

'Just because two chaps share digs doesn't mean they're queer' – Captain Bill Mitchell, secretary of the Sherlock Holmes society, as reported in the *Daily Mail*.

ISBN 0 85449 081 7   £3.95